SAVIDGE

Joe Savidge has revenge in his heart. But after he becomes involved in some dirty dealings, he's almost beaten to death and ends up in Pioche, Nevada, with little more than the shirt on his back. He meets a woman with a lucrative connection to a mysterious Frenchman. This provides him with the opportunity to purchase guns and horses: necessities for a man hell-bent on retribution. And all Savidge must do is lie in wait for destiny to arrive . . .

SEAN KENNEDY

SAVIDGE

Complete and Unabridged

LINFORD
Leicester

First published in Great Britain in 2010 by
Robert Hale Limited
London

First Linford Edition
published 2012
by arrangement with
Robert Hale Limited
London

British Library CIP Data

Kennedy, Sean, *1939* –
    Savidge.- -(Linford western library)
    1. Retribution- -Fiction. 2. Western stories.
    3. Large type books.
    I. Title II. Series
    823.9′2–dc23

    ISBN 978–1–4448–0987–9

Published by
F. A. Thorpe (Publishing)
Anstey, Leicestershire

Set by Words & Graphics Ltd.
Anstey, Leicestershire
Printed and bound in Great Britain by
T. J. International Ltd., Padstow, Cornwall

This book is printed on acid-free paper

For Ada Ellen Holmes

1

The two ladies lay seductively on their backs, smiling at the ceiling. The old man cast an appraising eye over their forms, shifting the remains of a long dead cigar across his mouth as he contemplated them with an almost lascivious intensity. He smiled. They sure were beautiful.

Then his remaining opponent flipped over his two knaves dismissively and the old man's smile widened as the beaten player grunted and stood up. He watched the younger man leave the table without a word, cross the boards and push through the batwings into the night air.

'Any more takers?' the old man said, a touch of triumph in his creaky voice as he scooped up his winnings.

A miner at the table said something about it being late and made his

goodnights. Another shrugged offhand-
edly and made for the bar.

The old-timer looked crestfallen.

Holiday Smith gathered the cards
and began shuffling them. Her eyes
twinkled as she nodded at the newly
acquired bills and coins that the
old-timer was stacking triumphantly
before him. Up till that last deal he had
been down to cents. 'Well,' she said, 'it's
getting late and I was leaving too. But,
if you can bluff everybody at the table
to pack in on just two queens with a pot
like that in the middle, I'm staying a
spell longer.'

The oldster's mahogany face, seemingly stained with at least sixty years'
sun, smoke and grime, cracked once
more into a smile. 'Name's Jed, ma'am.'

'Holiday Smith.'

'I know, ma'am,' he said. 'Everybody
in town knows Holiday Smith.'

Play resumed but his smile lessened
with successive deals and a half-hour on
she'd cleared him out bar a few dollars.
She didn't feel guilty. The old-timer had

come in with virtually nothing and made a stack. It was only that stack of which she had simply relieved him.

It was Friday night in The Golden Nugget Saloon, Pioche. Although the mining town's heyday was now past, there was still enough money flowing around on pay night for the atmosphere to be convivial.

'Easy come, easy go,' the oldster sighed, as the lady claimed the last of the coinage.

'That's real philosophical of you, Jed,' she said. 'Hope you've enjoyed yourself is all.'

He suddenly grimaced and closed his eyes.

'You all right, pa?' she asked.

'Comes and goes,' he said. He attempted a chuckle and added, 'Like the money — comes and goes. I'll be OK in a minute, ma'am.'

'I'll get you a drink,' she said. 'Maybe that will help.'

By the time she had returned with his refilled tankard, for which he thanked her, he had brightened up enough to suggest, 'One more game, ma'am?'

She shook her head. 'When you've finished that, old-timer, I figure you'd be better off heading for home and bed. Anyway, by my reckoning you've got two dollars left. Best leave with something in your pocket. The way the cards have been running for me the last hour, I'd only take that from you too.'

'I'll take that chance. Like you say, Holiday, I'm enjoying myself. An interesting game of chance and the company of an attractive woman an' all. By Jiminy, what more could a man ask?'

'You sure?'

He nodded.

She pushed the deck forward. 'OK, cut for deal.'

It wasn't long before she'd cleared him out yet again; this time completely.

'I did warn you,' she said.

His glum face suddenly lit up. 'You take non-American specie?'

She looked quizzical. 'Maybe. Depends.'

His old fingers worked through

tattered pockets until he came up with a coin which he pushed across the table. 'I was forgetting about this,' he said. 'Carried it for quite a spell now. One of my lucky tokens, you might call it.' He laughed. 'Hell, don't know why I say that. Never brought me any luck!'

She picked it up and examined it.

'It's gold,' he claimed. 'Pure gold.'

'I'll take your word for it,' she said, as she tried to read the buffed lettering. 'Too worn for me to read. But don't look Spanish. And it certainly ain't English.'

Due to the tight money policies of the Eastern banks the demand for tender out West fell short of the needs of an expanding economy such as that on the frontier. As a result other currencies were in circulation at the fringes, primarily Spanish dollars; while English guineas and pounds were no exception. And the further north-west you went, Russian roubles could surface. In some establishments in the more cosmopolitan of towns there was even a blackboard with current exchange rates chalked upon it.

So there was nothing out of the ordinary in the appearance of strange currency in this way. Indeed, in her own trade Holiday was accustomed on occasion to contemplate the acceptance of non-US tender. But she had never seen anything like this piece.

'Gold, you say?'

She tried it in her teeth. 'OK,' she concluded. 'I feel benevolent. Say on par with five dollars?'

'I ain't no specialist, ma'am, but sounds good enough for me.' He nodded at his cards. 'Now yours truly is liquid again,' he continued, ' — up five dollars, ma'am.'

And the coin joined the rest of his stake.

'I've got a good hand,' she said by way of warning, and added five dollars.

He whistled.

'Sorry to do this to you, Jed, but you're gonna need another five dollars to see me. That's money you ain't got.'

His whistle turned into a loud tuneless exhalation of air. Then: 'Wait a minute.' He scrabbled through his pockets again and eventually came up with another of his strange coins.

Holiday raised a hand. 'Hang on there, pal. How many of those damn things have you got? A favour is a favour but there is a limit.'

'Just the two, ma'am. Honest. That one you took and this.'

'You sure?'

'Yeah.'

'OK.'

'Same rate?'

'If you insist.'

He flipped the coin onto the table. 'Right, Miss Holiday. There you are: five dollars to see you.'

She resisted allowing triumph to enter her voice. 'Sorry, my friend. My flush beats your three.'

He shook his head as she pulled the money in. 'Ma'am, you can sure play a hand of cards.'

'I never said I was a beginner.'

He pushed back his chair in preparation to be on his way. 'I'll take my leave, ma'am, and thank you for the pleasure of your company.'

'Let me stand you to a drink before you go.'

He looked surprised. 'Like you said a whiles back, ma'am — if you insist!' She smiled and led him towards the bar.

He dropped his cigar butt in a fat brass cuspidor as he bellied up to the counter and she eased herself onto a rump-polished stool. 'Whiskey for me, Sam,' she said as she crooked her elbows on the bar, 'and whatever my friend here is having.'

'Coming up, Miss Holiday,' the barman said, reaching for the relevant bottle. 'The usual it is.'

She opened her purse and took out the foreign coins. 'You take these, Sam? Worth at least five dollars apiece. You can keep the change.'

'And I can keep the change!' the man scoffed. 'Do me a favour, Holiday. You know I'm an employee here. Ain't within my purview to make decisions on such things. If the books ain't right at the end of the night, the boss takes it out of my wages.'

'Be it on your head, Sam,' she said, returning them to her purse and rooting through it to get something more acceptable. 'But I reckon you've just given up the chance of getting your hands on an heirloom you could pass on to your kids.'

'Ain't got no kids, Miss Holiday. An' if I did, don't think they'd thank me for something like that.'

* * *

A little later she was back in the lobby of The Overlander, the local joy house that she ran. But business was not good. The piano, unplayed since she'd reluctantly discharged her regular piano player, stood silent and one of her two remaining girls was seated in the darkened room, looking rather disconsolate.

'Bad night, Mary?' Holiday asked.

'Yes, ma'am. Only a couple of johns since you left.'

The proprietor recognized the derby on the hat stand. 'And one of them's Sam Hedley by the look of it.'

'Yes, ma'am,' the young girl said, raising her eyes to the ceiling, indicating the customer's upstairs location. 'Ethel's entertaining him now.'

Holiday shook her head. 'Quiet, eh? Wages night too. Bad sign. Oh well, can't be helped. You're not to blame.'

She dropped on the settee and looked around the quiet, sad room. Gone were the days when she had had ten girls or more on the books, good-looking and clean. Plus, her place had been known for the best card game in Pioche and her bar renowned for the quality of its liquor. And that had been her hallmark — quality in whatever she supplied. You could get liquor at other places. In Tent City, the large section of town made up of ramshackle shacks and tents where folk in decent clothes didn't go, a guy could have his choice from a large number of women for a dollar and a bellyful of rotgut drink for less. But she catered for those who wanted class.

She sighed and tried to shake off the nostalgia. That was then, she told herself, and this was now.

As is the eventual fate of any town whose sole *raison d'etre* was an exhaustible resource, Pioche's boom days were over. The once astronomic returns from investments in mining had now settled down to an average for any business Averagetown, USA. And, with averageness, came the need for respectability: churches, chapels and morals committees.

After a while she heard feet on the landing and looked up to see Ethel arm in arm with her 'guest'.

'Evening, Holiday,' Hedley said, as he descended the stairs and caught sight of the proprietor. The town butcher, he had become a regular and valued client at the establishment since his wife had died.

'Evening, Sam.'

He retrieved his hat from the stand, and was suddenly hit by a thought which prompted him to cross over to Holiday and sit beside her.

'Thought you'd like to know. I been hearing things. Bad news I'm afraid.'

Sam Hedley was a fount of town knowledge. Everybody needed meat and a large section of the town's population passed through his store on a weekly basis. The result was there wasn't much that went on in the town that he didn't know about. He had a good idea of who was who, and who did what and to whom. Moreover, his knowledge was democratic, stretching from the town muckamucks down to the inhabitants of the seamy Tent City quarter.

'From the chatter I been hearing,' he went on in a low, conspiratorial tone, 'the committee are getting more energetic.'

The women of the town had formed what they called the 'Upholding of Moral Values' committee. At first Holiday hadn't been concerned because it all seemed like the kind of inconsequential bluster she had been used to in other towns where she'd operated. But in time the actions of the good ladies of Pioche had started to take effect and she had begun to lose important customers, starting with town dignitaries. It had got to the point where her clientele was now a mere dribble, consisting of drunken miners who had rarely been in the market for The Overlander's quality services, and through travellers, of which the town didn't have many these days.

'They're pressing for more action on The Overlander,' he concluded.

'More action? They've managed to deter most of my customers already! Isn't that enough for them?'

'Fact is, Holiday, from the way they're talking they're not going to be happy until they've closed your place down. I'm not party to their decision, you understand — just letting you know.'

She patted his arm. 'Thanks, Sam.'

'Night.'

She followed him to the door and looked along the street to check if there might be any late customers. But this side of the tarpaper shanties the town was empty.

'May as well get yourselves some shuteye,' she said to the girls after she had locked the door. 'See you in the morning.'

She dropped into a seat and watched them make their way up the stairs.

For a while she pondered on her circumstances. She was a gambling woman and loved cards. For a long time she had run a permanent game in her establishment. Not only had the players been well heeled but the game was good for business as it could be used as an excuse by those who needed one. When confronted by an irate wife over his attendance at such a place of notoriety, a public figure could always claim he'd only gone there for a game of cards as it was well known that Holiday ran the best game in town

— above board, gentlemanly and no shoot-outs. But since the committee had begun to turn on the screws, those days were fast becoming a mere memory.

Which is how come she was reduced to getting her gambling kicks and social diversions at small time games like the one that evening in The Golden Nugget saloon.

But the way things were going, it wouldn't be long before she would be hard pushed to find the stake for even those penny-ante games.

After a while she doused the lights, went upstairs and lay on her bed in the dark, relaxing in the afterglow of drink and an evening of good fellowship, a state rapidly becoming difficult for her to attain.

2

A solid-built man, a shade above average height, heavy-footed along the rutted trail towards the small cluster of shacks around a stamp mill that called itself Bullionville. Joe Savidge was weary after a long shift hacking at the face in the depths of the mine where he had been working for the last couple of weeks.

'Hey, Joe! Get your rump up here and take the weight off your legs.'

He turned to see a ramshackle buckboard drawing up beside him, a wizened Shoshoni hauling on the ribbons.

'Flying Dog!' the younger man said, with pleasure in his voice.

He jumped up and the driver nudged the ancient horse into motion.

Savidge had been working for a small operation out in Dry Lake Valley but had been laid off when the lode became exhausted. He'd trudged the byways, eventually turning up at Bullionville where he'd managed to find similar work. But, without much cash, it had not been easy to get accommodation. Flying Dog had a small shack on the edge of town where he lived with his Mexican wife and, hearing of Savidge's difficulty, had offered him a bed at their place. At the time the Indian had suggested that it might do until the young man got to know the town and had time to find something more acceptable.

But in no time at all, Savidge had become partial to the Mexican cooking of the old man's missus and enjoyed the couple's company such that he had put no effort into finding further lodgings.

'What brings you out here?' he asked, as the wagon rattled along the meagre road towards the town.

The Indian nodded back at his load.

Savidge turned in his seat and appraised the wagon's contents behind him.

'Been busy I see.'

'Collecting firewood,' the Indian said. 'Caught a couple of jacks too. Hope you like rabbit stew.'

'Nothing better. Brung up on it.'

When they made town Savidge pointed at the rough shack labelled Eldorado Saloon. 'I need to replace a day's sweat,' he said. 'I reckon you do too. Join me in a drink?'

'It's better I didn't, Joe. The way things are.'

'Oh, come on, pa. Wielding an axe in the sun and chasing rabbits through the dust out there you could benefit from wetting your whistle; you know you could.'

And, before the old man could demur further, Savidge had pulled on the ribbons. When the wagon crunched to a standstill he gestured for the old man to pull on the handbrake.

That done, they dropped down, crossed to the saloon and entered.

As he pushed through the batwings, Savidge recognized the owner at the

18

end of the bar. You didn't have to live long in town to know who Leo Fage was — the town's big cheese with interests extending beyond the Eldorado; interests in the shape of extorting fees from all the town's businesses. To aid him in this he had two henchmen: a grizzled old-timer and a hard-headed youngster. He was rarely seen without them and they were there now.

A hardcase trio against whom there was nobody in town with the guts to say them nay.

At the back of the room a big faro wheel turned. Blackjack tables were on either side and there was a scattering of poker tables around the rest of the room. Miners had money and Fage saw it as one of his missions in life to take it off them, along with soaking the storekeepers with his protection racket.

Savidge ordered two beers.

The bartender looked over Savidge's shoulder at his companion. 'No Indians.'

'All we want is a beer,' Savidge said.

'It's been hot out there.'

'You heard the man,' Fage shouted from the end of the bar. 'No redskins. Company policy. They smell the place up especially when they been sweating in the sun.'

'It's all right,' Flying Dog whispered, tugging his companion's elbow. 'Let's not cause trouble.'

Savidge turned to see the old man heading back to the door. He looked back at the bartender and said, 'Well, *I'm* thirsty. Thirsty enough for two beers.'

The bartender cast a glance along the bar at Fage who nodded somewhat unenthusiastically.

Savidge dropped coins on the bar and took the drinks outside. 'Does that happen often?' he asked, nodding back at the saloon as he handed a brimming glass to his friend.

The Indian downed a thirst-quenching draught, then removed his headband and proceeded to wipe his face and brow with it. 'Don't know, Joe,' he said, as he replaced his headgear. 'Ain't never been in before.'

'Gee, I'm sorry. I wouldn't have subjected you to that if I'd known. As you know, I ain't been in town long.'

'I'm used to it. Way of the world.'

Savidge grunted and added, 'Huh, the *white* man's world.'

The old man smiled, as though at some knowledge they shared, and they finished their drinks quietly.

'Come on, pardner,' Savidge said finally. 'Let's get our hides over to some place where the air is cleaner. I'm real looking forward to that rabbit stew.'

3

Everybody knew when Holiday Smith was going shopping. In public she didn't have to sashay around ostentatiously to be noticed. Love her or hate her, no observer could simply ignore her. Passing women would raise their noses sniffily. Husbands greeted her sheepishly — or looked away awkwardly, dependent on whether they were in the company of their wives at the time. On the other hand unattached miners greeted her raucously by name.

And so it was that hot morning in Pioche, under a bonnet to protect her delicate skin from the strong glare, and shawl draped decorously round her shoulders, she strolled along the boardwalk under a sun that was reaching its noonday peak.

The manager of the general store looked askance as she entered. It was not that he didn't want her trade — she was a good customer — but the problem was she deterred others. Like now. As she presented herself at the counter and asked for a pound of coffee beans, the two browsing women already in there threw sniffy glances at each other, muttered something unintelligible, then made for the door.

'Don't worry, Mr Prendergast,' Holiday said with a smile. 'I'll make it quick and be on my way.'

'Pay them no never-mind, Miss Holiday,' he said, as he picked up a scoop and moved along the counter to the scales. 'And what else can I do for you this beautiful day?'

After the coffee she bought some soap, several cans of peaches and a handful of other sundries before returning to the sunlight.

Her purchases complete, she headed back to The Overlander and sighed in quiet irritation when she saw who was sitting under the awning.

The mayor.

'Good morning, Holiday,' he said, touching his expensive Chicago-bought hat.

'Good morning, Mr Grade.'

'Please, it's Bartholomew — or better still, Bart.'

'I know. You have told me many times, Mr Grade.'

He looked upset that she persisted in addressing him by surname. 'Can we talk?' he asked.

'We really don't have anything to talk about.' She passed inside and placed her bag on a chair. 'Now, if you'll excuse me.' She took off her bonnet, shaking her head to fluff out her hair, knowing full well he had followed her into the lobby.

'Just give me a chance, Holiday.'

'I really don't see the point, Mr Mayor.'

For months he had beleaguered her. If only she would accept him, he'd whined, they would be so happy together. Not only mayor, he was a reasonably wealthy man with mining interests and so had the wherewithal to provide for her, he had argued. And then the corniest bit of all: he could take her away from all this.

Trouble was he overlooked one thing: she couldn't stand the sight of him. Along with his physical unattractiveness, she had known him long enough to know he was as two-faced and oily as they came.

'I truly wish you would reconsider my offer, ma'am,' he said, hat now held deferentially before him.

'I really don't know how to bring a halt your persistence without hurting your feelings,' she said. 'The fact is, Mr Grade, a woman knows when things might stand a chance of working, and I know there can be nothing between us.'

'I beg you,' he said, his hat brim now being worked feverishly through his fingers, 'simply to give me a chance. It's all I ask.'

'Now, you must excuse me, I do have things to do,' she said, draping her shawl over the back of the chair and picking up her bag.

'Is that your last word?' he prompted, his tone hardening as she examined the items of her shopping in seeming obliviousness to his presence.

'Yes. Last, final, absolute. How can I say it? And I do wish you wouldn't continually pester me in this way.'

Something in what she said lit a fuse and it took a moment for him to regain his composure. 'Pester?' he said finally. 'So that's how you see it. A man of my stature — and you dismiss me as pestering.'

He paused, churning things over in his mind. 'Right.' He rammed on his hat and returned to the door. 'You'll learn how powerful I am, Miss Holiday Smith — or Miss Whatever-your-real-name-is.'

He paused again after he had opened the door and swept a hand around the lobby. 'This precious place of yours for a start. You'll find to your cost what happens to those who cross Bartholomew Grade. Don't say I didn't warn you.'

When the door crashed shut behind him she dropped onto the chair and sighed. An attractive woman, she was no stranger to the matter of declining a suitor. Of course, she knew how powerful the man was. Which is why she knew it had been especially important that in his case she had done her best to drop him down gently.

But she also knew he was the kind who didn't cotton to 'No' for an answer.

4

'I'm bored, Leo.'

Leo Fage looked every inch the businessman that he made himself out to be in his dark suit with gold fob chain stretching across his vest front. He leant back in his boardwalk chair in the front of the Eldorado Saloon and appraised the speaker, a young man whose horse-like face was looking more mournful than usual. 'If I had a cent for every time you've said that, Link, I'd be a rich man.'

'Rich man? You don't do so bad, Leo.'

That was true. Fage, along with his two henchmen, ran the Eldorado as well as the town's protection racket. Having established a reputation for violence, all that was required was to take a weekly stroll round the town's businesses and collect their money.

'I don't know what to say, Link. You don't have to work hard. I give you a good cut of the action. Hell, what more could you want?'

Link Turner looked up and down the town's main drag in which he was standing. 'I've sampled all the delights in this place. A guy needs variety.'

He had a case. Bullionville was a very small mining town and had little to offer a man who had a craving for perpetual novelty and stimulation.

He clumped up onto the boardwalk and dropped his rear into the seat beside his boss. 'I've sampled all the liquor. And had the ass of every woman ten times over — if I bother to count. Hell, there's nothing else left.'

'Can't have everything,' Fage said. 'We got a good number here. Won't find such an easy state of affairs anywhere else. OK, it's not Denver or Frisco but money-wise you don't want for a damn thing.'

'Yeah,' said the third man who was sitting on the boardwalk edge, cleaning a Winchester while puffing on a cherrywood pipe. 'Gotta take the rough with the smooth.' Name of Gelder and the oldest, he saw himself as the philosopher of the trio.

'It's all right for you,' Link grumbled. 'You're so old you're past it.'

Gelder stiffened and took the pipe out of his mouth. 'You come over here. I'll show you who's past it.'

'Don't invite trouble, Grandpa. You know I'd flatten you — '

His talking was cut short by the oldster whirling round, Winchester aimed threateningly. 'You think so, younker?' he snapped, jabbing the gun forward. 'There's more'n two ways of skinning a cat. At this range I could split you in half with this before there was anything you could do about it.'

Turner chuckled. 'That don't scare me. Even an old man like you ain't crazy enough to clean a Winchester while it's loaded.'

Gelder frowned at the exposure of his bluff.

'Cut it out, you two,' Fage said.

'You ain't got my needs, is all I'm saying,' Turner said. 'My nature is I gotta have excitement.'

The old man laid his gun on the boards and tossed his tobacco pouch towards him. 'Here, roll yourself a smoke. Maybe that'll satisfy a craving. At least with something in your mouth you might not whine so much.'

After he had built a cigarette for himself and lit it, the younger man returned the makings and slumped onto the boardwalk's edge, feet planted in the dust.

With little sound other than that of flies buzzing and Gelder tinkering with his long-barrelled firearm, it remained that way until Turner spotted an elderly Indian walking down the drag. He waited until the man was level then flicked his finished cigarette butt so that it bounced off the Indian's jacket in a shower of sparks. The old man paused, looked at the trio then made to continue on his way.

But Turner leapt up and sprinted out into the drag to block the man's progress. 'Where do you think you're going?'

'Want no trouble. Just going home.'

'Sounds to me like that's just what you're looking for — trouble. Not addressing me as 'sir' and all.'

The Indian toyed nervously with the beads of his necklace. 'Just going home, sir.'

'Not yet you're not,' the young man said, his eyes burning with contempt. 'First you're gonna provide us with some entertainment, a commodity this burg's very short on.'

He looked at his friends. 'Any ideas, boys?'

'Tell you what,' Gelder said. 'I heard a lot about the redskins' Ghost Dance but I've never seed it. Tell him to give us a sample.'

'It is a religious ritual, sir,' the Indian said. 'Very elaborate and not to be scoffed at.'

'Ghost Dance, eh?' Turner said. 'Now I am intrigued. Give us an exhibition.'

'It invokes spirits, sir. Not to be scorned or treated lightly.'

'I've had enough talk,' the young man said. 'Show me.' With that he pulled his gun and planted a couple of rounds close to the Indian's feet.

★ ★ ★

Sitting in the Eldorado, Joe Savidge finished his drink, replenishing the sweat he had expended during his shift working at the face, and headed for the batwings. He was just emerging into the sunlight when he was staggered by very loud gunshots. Some punk kid was firing at the feet of an Indian immobilized in the middle of the drag.

He knew the redman. It was Flying Dog, the respected elder who owned the shack were he boarded. He also knew the perpetrators: the Fage gang who effectively ruled the town. The punk kid was Link Turner. And enjoying the spectacle was Leo Fage himself.

Savidge threw a glance at the law

office. But he figured it would be unlikely there would be any help from that source. Luke Granger, the constable funded by the mining companies, was a good man but a man who realized he was only in place as a figurehead. He was probably peering from behind the curtains at this very moment, having long realized that, singlehanded, he was no match for the Fage bunch. It was clear to anyone in town with half an eye — even to a newcomer like Joe Savidge — that the constable always displayed a habit of giving them a wide berth.

The hothead let loose with another couple of shots and the Indian began to move his feet.

He don't deserve this treatment, Savidge concluded to himself. *Fact is, nobody does. But what to do?*

Then: *What the hell*, he decided, and strode towards the scene. He unclipped the pick hanging from his belt and gripped the handle, keeping the tool out of sight behind him as he advanced.

'You want to make somebody dance?'

34

he said up close. 'Try me.'

Turner grinned, noting the dusted-up features of the speaker. 'Anything to oblige, muck-shifter.' And he triggered a shot between Savidge's feet. The miner raised his foot as though to start some dance but it was in fact a step — a planned step — a step that took him straight up to the face of the young man.

And his hand whipped round to the front.

'This is a miner's pick pressing up into your stomach. Feel the point? You've only got one shot left. I've been counting. Try to use it on me, or make some other sudden movement, and you'll be opened up from gut to gizzard. I've had a long, hard day and I ain't got much patience.' Without taking his eyes from those of the young man he added, 'Get yourself home, old-timer.'

Staring close-up into the young Turner's face, Savidge waited to hear evidence of the Indian's departure.

35

'Flying Dog, are you on your way?'

'Yeah, Joe.'

Suddenly Savidge's head jarred. From his position on the sidewalk Gelder had flung the Winchester he had been cleaning. Hurled butt-first with as much force as the old man could muster, it was enough to send Savidge staggering sidewards; and enough for Turner to club him with his own weapon so that he pitched into the sand. Still dazed, Savidge was vaguely aware of the young man ramming his revolver hard against his throat. 'You interfering bastard, I'll teach you to shove your nose where it ain't wanted.'

Now in a mindless frenzy, Turner grabbed the fallen Winchester near its muzzle-end and stood up to tower over the grounded man. With two hands on the barrel he used it as a club, swinging it in a wide arc to crunch sickeningly against the side of Savidge's head.

He laughed at the blood-splattering effect. And the little grasp on reality that Savidge had had after the first blows, now dissipated completely.

Gelder jumped away from the board-walk on his ungainly legs and wrenched his gun from the young man's grip. 'That ain't no way to treat a Winchester.'

'Did the trick, didn't it, though?'

'The apple of me eye, this is,' the old man said, examining his weapon for damage. 'You younkers ain't got no respect.'

Turner grinned. 'Hey, you was the one who flung your precious gun halfway across the street.'

'Well . . .'

The young man's attention turned to the Indian who was now some yards away with his face voided by what he had seen.

'Now where was we?' Turner shouted, slipping new loads into his revolver. 'Oh, yes, you were entertaining us.'

The old man backed some more, then turned and began to move away as quickly as his arthritic legs would allow him.

Turner laughed at the spectacle for a moment, then recommenced firing.

Suddenly the man pitched forward into the sand.

'Hell,' the young man said, staring at the grounded figure. 'The old buzzard's fainted. Inconsiderate bastard's deprived me of some more fun.'

Gelder gently laid down his precious gun on the boards and strolled casually over to the still form. Then he looked back. 'He ain't fainted. One of your bullets went astray, Link. Got him in the back.' He looked closer. 'Smack in the pumper, judging by the way the red stuff's gushing out.'

The three men returned to the boardwalk and sat down. Fage lit a cigar, the other two put together cigarettes. As they smoked they contemplated the two sprawled-out figures.

'What shall we do with them, boss?' Gelder asked after a time.

'No rush,' Fage said. 'Them lying in the street like that for a spell is good for business. It'll remind townsfolk we ain't to be messed with.'

★ ★ ★

It was quiet again save for the buzzing of flies. Occasionally someone would appear from a doorway, take general stock of the situation and return indoors or go quietly about their business.

A half-hour on, a buckboard came trundling into view. Its driver saw the bodies and manoeuvred the horses around them, like they were some everyday obstacles that one might find in the street. He had also seen the Fage bunch and thought better of making any comment.

Fage hailed the man. 'Where you headed, pardner?'

'Pioche, sir. Delivering mining gear.'

'Pull in here a spell,' Fage said, and stepped into the drag, gesturing for his cronies to follow him. 'Got some extra deliveries for you, pilgrim.'

He pushed a bill into the driver's hand and pointed to the still figures. 'Two in fact. A dead Indian. Dump him anywhere you see fit. Don't matter where as long as it's far enough away so that his smell don't reach town. The grubby miner — he's as close to dead as dammit with the head pounding he's took — take him the full distance and drop him off at Pioche.' He laughed raucously. 'Huh, he should be dead by then, anyhows.'

The man didn't argue. Like anybody else in town, he knew better than to cross the Fage bunch — as the new load of freight now being loaded into his wagon testified.

5

It was a sunny morning. Holiday Smith
was out back toiling over a washtub.
Regular washing went along with the
staining of bedsheets being an occupa-
tional feature. She had been up since
first light and the clothesline was
already full. It had been some time
since she had been able to afford to
send garments and linen to the laundry.
Inside the building, her two remaining
girls were on cleaning tasks as she had
long had to dispense with the services
of domestic staff too.

'Mr Wyler for you, ma'am.'

She turned to see one of her girls,
broom in hand, at the back door.

'Thank you, Mary.'

The girl stood aside to allow The Overlander's owner to step out into the sun.

'Good morning, Mr Wyler,' Holiday
said, straightening up from her chores

and wiping hair out of her eyes with the back of her wrist. 'I hope you haven't come for the rent. It's a little early for that and I don't have it to hand.'

'Indeed, it is not yet due,' her landlord said. 'But when I say that *that* is not the purpose of my visit, do not allow your spirits to rise. I am the bearer of some graver news.'

'And that is?'

'I'll come straight to the point, ma'am. I'm afraid you have two weeks to vacate the premises.'

'Can't say I wasn't expecting something like this. Don't the do-gooders realize that closing my place will not put an end to the provision of womanly comfort to men in the town? Fellers will always get what they want and there are always women who are willing to provide it.'

'The way of the world, Holiday, but we are pawns.'

'A man wants a quick grope he goes to Tent City,' she said. 'Your pious league will never get rid of that.' Tent

City was the name of the town's rough quarter, consisting of a mess of tents, shacks and lean-tos, that had made its appearance on day one of the very first regular mining operation on the site that eventually was to become Pioche.

The man shrugged apologetically.

'It's a fact of life,' she added by way of emphasis, 'there are times when a man wants the open thighs of a willing woman. The tarpaper shanties provide it, so do I. The big difference is I provide quality.'

'That's the whole point, Holiday. The genteel folk can see your place. Stands brazen on the main drag. They can't see the shenanigans that go on in the unrefined section. The ladies of the committee never go there.'

She dropped onto a stool by the side of the tub. 'I suppose I don't have to ask what spurs you to this decision.'

'Yes. It's the committee.'

'Of course. And I suppose the mayor had nothing to do with it?'

He grimaced, reflecting he didn't

want to pursue that theme. 'They gave me the order this morning.'

'And you have to do as they say?'

'Life would be very difficult for me should I act counter to their wishes. You'll understand that.'

'Yes, not to mention the mayor.' She paused, then added, 'I understand, Mr Wyler. You know on which side your bread's buttered.'

'Anyways, they came round as a delegation first thing. I came over immediately to pass on the news. I thought it only proper to give you enough time as I could for you to arrange your affairs.'

'Not much to arrange. I can get everything I own into a carpetbag.'

'They stipulated a mere week but I persuaded them to extend to two. And, in the circumstances, we'll forgo any outstanding rent.'

'Thank you for that.'

'It's the least I can do. I'm sorry.'

'Well, thank you for your expedition and courtesy.'

★ ★ ★

Later in the day she was wrapping up the accounts. She opened the cash-box and took out what she owed the girls. She contemplated what remained: enough to buy passage for herself out of town and to see her through a month or two. Under the circumstances she couldn't count on adding much to the amount before she left.

She took out the two foreign coins she had picked up the night before. It was the first time she'd seen them in daylight. She took them to the window and studied them in turn. In the bright sun she could make out some of the lettering. She knew enough of the language to recognize it as French.

She examined the effigy. Looked like Napoleon; complete with the laurel wreath around his head that he had donned with his own hands when proclaiming himself as emperor.

She went to her bureau, laid the coins on the top and rooted through the drawers until she found a card. She sat down. It was the first time she had read it.

Anton Valeur, an historian from some academy in Paris, writing a book about French immigration to America. He'd stayed for a few days at The Overlander some weeks back. With her normal business in the doldrums she hadn't been in a position to turn up her nose at the provision of straightforward accommodation for the right person.

With his European manners, he had brought a touch of class to the place and she had been fascinated by him. He was specifically interested in the Napoleonic period and, in passing, he had asked her to let him know if any coins from that epoch should turn up.

She re-read the details he had penned at the bottom of the card giving the place — a hotel in Cedar City — where he could be contacted while he was still in the region. If he hadn't moved on he was still only a stagecoach ride fiom Pioche.

At such a time, with her life being in turmoil, she would have normally pushed the thing out of her mind, but he'd been such a pleasant and polite gentleman. What made him stand out in her memory especially was that he was a card player and she recalled several agreeable sessions that stretched into the early morning playing two-handers, including French games such as piquet and ecarte that he taught her. Yes, the least she could do for such a charming gentleman was to let him know about the two samples that had come into her possession.

She thought upon it. She needed to go to the stores shortly and the telegraph office would not be out of her way. Resolving to use the occasion to send him a wire, she slipped the card into the pocket on her dress.

Then, in her eventual cable she offered to post the coins to save him journeying out again. After all, they were of little use to her.

* * *

The first thing of which Savidge was aware when he came to was that his head felt like it had spent time under a stampede. For a spell the throbbing in his skull drove everything from his brain. Then he sensed the jolting of planking beneath him. It was dark. He could hear wheels turning, the clop of hoofs. He extended his arms sideways. On his right he felt the side of a buckboard, on the left some kind of load. Bags, something metal, machinery perhaps.

If this was a wagon, there had to be a driver. He hauled himself to a sitting position and grasped the side to steady himself.

'Hey, what's going on? Where am I?'

The wagon slowed, stopped. Ahead somebody dropped down.

Then he heard a voice. 'I thought it best to leave you be, mister. You were out cold. Thank God one of you's OK.'

'One? What the hell you talking about?'

'The other one. Dead.'

Savidge looked around the wagon in the moonlight, then under the tarp. 'What other one?'

'Ain't there no more. Dropped the remains off like I was told.'

'Help me down.'

'If you can work your way along towards the back of the wagon, I'll drop the backboard. It'll be easier.'

A minute later Savidge was sitting on a grassy slope, nursing his head. 'Tell me the story.'

'I run a freighting business out of Bullionville. Only one wagon but it puts bread on the table. I'd loaded up with mining gear and some supplies for Pioche, and was heading out of town. Got stopped by Mr Fage.'

'You know him then?'

'Everybody in Bullionville knows Fage. Anyways, there were two bodies — I reckoned they was dead — lying in the middle of the street for everybody to see. His boys loaded them in back, told me to get rid of 'em.'

He paused and for a moment the only sound was that of bugs in the darkness. 'If you know Fage,' he continued, 'you'll know he's not somebody you argue with. I got a wife and kid to think of. So didn't ask any questions. One guy was obviously dead and I figure Fage reckoned you were past recovery.'

Savidge worked his neck one way then the other, his brain still numb with a pounding ache. 'The way I feel I might be.'

'When I disposed of the Indian — '

'Indian? What Indian? You mean Flying Dog?'

'Don't know his name. An old guy.'

'And you say he was dead?'

'Yeah, shot in the back. Judging by the amount of blood, the slug must have got him smack in the heart.'

'The bastards,' Savidge whispered low to himself, 'couldn't let the matter go until they'd killed him.'

'So, when I dumped the Indian — '

'Dumped him? Just like that? Jeez, he

was a pal of mine.'

'Goddamn, mister, I wasn't to know that. Judas Priest, I'm an ordinary guy minding my own business, going about doing my job and I get saddled with obligations imposed by the town's big piece of news in a suit. What the hell could I do, mister? And I didn't just dump the old feller, not like that. I treated his remains with due respect.'

'OK, go on.'

'Well, I checked you and found you were breathing. Figured best to get you somewhere where you can be looked after.'

'That'd be Pioche, I suppose.'

'Yeah.'

'How far now?'

The man pointed into the distance. 'Nearly there. Look, you can see the lights at the end of the valley.'

'OK. Help me up into the seat.'

When they were both seated up front, Savidge asked, 'He pay you for your night's work?'

The man looked sheepish. 'Yeah.'

'And how come you're running your business into the night?'

'Got a full workload over the next few days.' He gestured back with his thumb. 'Then a mining company in Pioche cabled they wanted this stuff brought over urgent. I need the work and the only way I could fit it into my schedule was to make it an evening delivery.'

Savidge focused his eyes on the faraway lights. 'Well, you may as well fulfil your part of the bargain with Fage and take me to the terminus. Seeing my passage has already been paid for.'

★   ★   ★

'This is as good as any,' Savidge said, when they got to the edge of town near an imposing building with the appearance of a hotel, glass-fronted door and all.

'This is the plush end of town,' the driver said. 'As a miner you might feel more at home in the mining end of

52

town. Just shacks and stuff. Locals call it Tent City.'

'This'll do. I can work my way through the town. It'll give me a chance to get my bearings.'

'OK, if you say so.'

The driver reined in the animals and his reluctant passenger eased himself down.

'You OK, mister?' the man said. 'You look a little shaky.'

'Apart from being a little dizzy, groggy in the legs and head thumping, I'm as fit as a fiddle.'

'Might be a good thing to see a doc now you're here.'

'I'll be all right,' Savidge said, as he took stock of his surroundings. Then: 'In the circumstances you'll understand my not saying thanks for the ride.'

'I'm sorry about all this, pal — what happened to you and you ending up in my wagon and all.'

'Don't worry. You were an innocent party in the caper.'

'You going back to Bullionville?'

53

'Nothing to go back for. Only been around a week or so. Still feeling my way about town. I'd worked a few shifts is all and pay was meagre.'

He straightened. 'What am I saying? I *do* have something to go back for. Some business needs attending to back there.' He felt his head again. 'As soon as I'm capable.' He thought on it. 'That reminds me, where exactly did you put the Indian down?'

'About halfway along the trail. While it was still light enough for me to see what I was doing.'

'In that case there'd be enough light for you to have noticed some feature nearby. Something striking that'll help me to locate the spot.'

'What for? You're not going back causing strife? Listen, feller, I don't want any trouble from Fage.'

'I've told you, the redskin was a pal of mine. So it's up to me to see he gets a decent resting place.'

The man saw the logic of it and cast his mind back. 'Laid the body in a dried-up creek on the left side of the trail. That's on the left heading this way.'

The wagoner thought some more. 'There was a big bluff on the right. Just after the trail narrows between a couple of crags.'

'Think that's enough for me to locate it?'

'Should be.'

The man looked at his former passenger, now swaying beside the wagon. 'Listen, how you doing for cash?'

'Got a few dollars.'

The driver pulled some crumpled bills from his shirt pocket. 'Here, take this. It's what Fage gave me. I'd only see it as blood money. I'd feel better if you had it. Anyways, reckon it'll be more use to you than me.'

Savidge took the money and looked at it in the moonlight. 'It's blood money all right, but in the circumstances . . . '

Then he shook the man's hand. 'Like I said, don't let this business be on your conscience. Nothing of it was your fault. See you around some time.'

The driver pulled away and Savidge gripped a stanchion for support. He threw a last glance at the wagon as it trundled towards the centre of town, then he heaved himself up onto the boardwalk. He looked along the drag with the intention of heading along it but his head started to swim again.

Coming over weak, he leant against the stanchion for a moment, and then tottered towards the nearest door.

6

Still dizzy, he brushed away the moths pestering his face as the creatures circled feverishly round the light coming through the glass, and he pushed open the door. There was no reception desk in the lobby just a woman in an ornate dress reclining on a *chaiselongue*; a good-looking woman.

And that was his last thought before he pitched forward onto the carpet.

He was vaguely aware of being helped to his feet, then over to the fancy seat.

'Like a room,' he said weakly.

'You need more than that, feller.'

Eyes closed, he wallowed in the woman's scent for moment.

'Like a room,' he repeated. 'If this place is not too pricey.'

'It's not a hotel.'

'Not a hotel,' he murmured. 'Sure looks like one. What kind of place is it?'

'Let's say it's a place where a guy pays a high rate for a room for a very short time.'

'High rate? Hey, I can't pay no high rate.' He pondered on the words, his brain fighting to make sense of things. 'Oh, one of those places,' he murmured eventually when things clicked. 'Sorry, ma'am. That kind of thing's not exactly what I'm looking for at the moment. Figure I'll be on my way.' He tried to rise but failed. 'Can you direct me to simple lodgings. Somewhere cheap.'

'Don't think you'd make it down the street, cowboy. You're in need of medical care as well as a room.'

'Don't want to put you to any inconvenience, ma'am.'

'I got time on my hands. At least let me clean you up. Rest here while I fetch a bowl of water.'

★ ★ ★

Minutes later he was laid out on the *chaise* with his head resting on a cushion. The woman was dabbing at his wounds with a cloth.

'You got a sizeable duck egg on the side of your head,' she said, 'you know that? And that's some nasty cut on the side of your forehead. That's what brawling in a Pioche saloon gets you.'

'Ain't been brawling. And ain't from Pioche.'

'Well, you sure had the tar whaled out of you someplace.'

'Bullionville. Got in short time ago.'

'Bullionville? That's just as lawless from what I hear.'

'And don't I know it?'

'So how did you get here?'

'Back of some freight wagon.'

She gently dabbed dry the injured areas. 'There. That's as much as I can do with what I've got.'

'And I thank you, ma'am. Now I gotta get going.'

'You're going nowhere, cowboy.'

'There you go, presuming again. I ain't a cowboy.'

'Never mind that. What matters is:

Holiday Smith ain't the kind of gal to turn away somebody in need and, feller, are you in need. So, my friend, I'm gonna get you upstairs and fetch a doctor. These injuries need checking properly and the right medication.'

'Can't afford no doctor, nor no fancy place like this.'

'Don't concern yourself with such matters. When the time comes I'm sure we'll be able to come to some mutually satisfactory arrangement.'

She eyed him and added, 'So you got a name?'

'Joe, ma'am. Joe Savidge.'

* * *

When he woke he was lying in a plush bed and his clothes had disappeared. He slipped his hand under the bedsheet and felt the length of his body. No underpants! He looked around but all that was available to cover his modesty was a frilly robe draped over a chair beside the bed. He could tell by the strength of light coming through the window that the day was well advanced.

He heaved himself to a sitting position at the side of the bed and groaned. His head was a shade better but he was still aware of its having being clobbered a few times.

He put fingers tenderly to the wounds. He could smell medication and vaguely recalled receiving the attentions of a doctor.

At the side of the room was a table bearing a pitcher and bowl. He hauled himself out of bed and, despite the fact there was nobody to see him, he pulled the bedsheet to his groin. Clumsily trailing the sheet he hobbled across the boards and splashed water over his face.

After towelling himself dry he looked in the dressing-table mirror. Angled his head this way and that, examining his injuries. Bad, but he'd had worse. Then he investigated the frilly gown more closely. Hell, it would barely cover what he wanted covering but, seeing no alternative, he pulled it on and made his way downstairs.

The woman, whom he recognized from the previous night, emerged from the kitchen, having heard his slow but noisy descent down the stairs. She watched him clutch the gown more tightly to him on sight of her.

'Don't have to be too coy, feller. I stripped you for bed so I'm familiar with your parts. Ain't nothing I ain't seen before.'

He looked sheepish. 'Hell, ma'am, don't remember that.'

'Reckon you don't remember much of anything. Anyways, how did you sleep?'

For the first time he noticed her voice carried a soft Southern slur.

'Pretty solid, ma'am.'

'Good, you needed it. The doc gave you a sedative.'

'The whole thing's a tad indistinct.'

He suddenly noticed two young women in the kitchen doorway giving him the once-over.

'These are Ethel and Mary,' Holiday

said. 'And this gentleman goes by the name of Joe.'

'Morning, ladies,' he said, pulling the gown closely to him again, an action that seemed to cause the girls to giggle.

'So what do you want for breakfast?' Holiday asked.

'Whatever's on the menu, ma'am. Thanks.'

Up till now he had not been in a position to assess his hostess physically. With his awareness of the world around him now much improved, he found her to be a fair woman, maybe in late thirties, easy on the eye.

'Where are my clothes?' he asked.

'On the line. Should be nearly dry by now.'

★ ★ ★

He wiped a hunk of bread round a greasy plate. 'That was sure good, ma'am. Ain't tasted the like for quite a spell.'

He stood up. 'My clothes dry yet?'

'Maybe. I'll check. But I hope you ain't fixing on leaving. You still need rest.'

'Got something that needs doing — pretty quick.'

'Like what?'

'Like a body that needs a decent burial.'

'Somebody you killed? Is that how come you staggered in here all beat up?'

'Staggering into town is part of it, but I didn't kill him. A friend of mine. He's lying somewheres along the trail back to Bullionville.' He told her the bones of the story.

'A brave thing to do,' she observed when he'd finished the account. 'Standing up to a bunch of hardcases like that.'

'I don't know about that, ma'am. I got a habit of doing first and thinking second. Acting on impulse I suppose you'd call it. Got me into trouble before now.'

'Still the action of a brave and honourable man.'

'So I need a horse to get out there and do the honours for my friend,' he said by way of conclusion. 'Trouble is I got little money to buy a mount or even hire one.'

'Leave it to me, Joe. I can still call in a favour. On one condition.'

'Go on.'

'Whatever you figure on doing, you leave the matter for a day. That head of yours has taken quite a knocking. I'm no sawbones but I reckon you need to get some more rest in before you apply yourself to anything strenuous.'

Savidge thought of his dead friend. 'It's hot out there, ma'am. Can't leave the business too long. I'll see how I feel this afternoon.'

He thought more on his planned task. 'And I need a shovel.'

'Shouldn't be a problem. This feller I'm thinking of, the one who's gonna lend me a horse, he'll have that too.'

He pushed away an empty plate. 'I'll see if my clothes are dry.'

'You're not putting on clean clothes till you've had a bath, mister. One of the rules of the house.'

★ ★ ★

While he was wallowing in the warm, soapy water of a tin bath, Holiday brought in a razor and shaving bowl. 'When you've done in there, this'll help you make yourself presentable.'

'What's shaving tackle doing in a houseful of women?'

'Never you mind.'

'My clothes?'

'Downstairs. Dry as a bone.'

He reached for a towel. 'Now if you don't mind, ma'am . . . '

She laughed as she went through the door. 'I do declare. Rare to get a feller as bashful as you in my line.'

As he dried himself he thought over the situation. He imagined Flying Dog's body lying forlorn and uncared for by the side of the trail. The sooner he got out there the better. Unpleasant things tended to happen very quickly to a body out in this heat. He would like to get the remains to the old-timer's widow but he knew such a task was beyond his present capability. But the way things were going, with this Holiday Smith getting the loan of a horse and shovel for him, he would be able to do something in the circumstances.

He mused on the woman's hospitality to him. Along with her getting him the loan of a horse and the way she was looking after him, he was building up quite a debt to the lady. How and when could he repay that?

'My, you look quite presentable,' she said when he finally emerged, once again fully dressed. There was something noble about his straight, almost patrician, nose and prominent cheekbones. 'Now you've got rid of all that grime and stubble. Quite a man, I do declare.'

In turn he looked at her. He noted the full mouth, the flourishing figure bursting the dress, the delicate hands. And that scent again. Heliotrope, he reckoned. Yes, and she was some woman.

7

Exhausted, Savidge sat slumped in the shade of an oak tree and looked at the mound a few yards from the dried-up creek. It was stacked with stones to deter animals. Ideally he would have liked to return the body of Flying Dog to his widow but he had had to take account of practicalities. He knew he wasn't yet up to such a task — or that of building a tree platform in the traditional way. With the body needing immediate attention the remaining option was a white-man type burial.

In riding out to the spot Savidge had almost fallen out of the saddle. His head was still prone to spinning. Then, wielding the shovel and burying the old man's remains had used up whatever energy he'd got left. Even if he had managed to make it to Bullionville there would have been the problem of

Flying Dog being an Indian. For that reason the fellow couldn't have been buried in the local cemetery and the way folks thought about such things someone would have even complained about his being buried within town limits; or anywhere near.

Eventually he dragged himself to his feet and stood before the heap of newly turned soil, with stacked rocks, on top of which he had laid Flying Dog's bead necklace.

He mumbled some fitting words he remembered from his childhood, words that Flying Dog would have understood. He picked up the Indian's headband in which he'd wrapped the man's few belongings, and tottered towards the waiting horse.

At least he'd done the decent thing. First opportunity he would tell the widow what he'd done and where her husband lay, and pass on to her the pathetic bundle.

★　★　★

Back at The Overlander, Savidge was noticeably quiet during the first meal following his return.

'Must have been very unpleasant,' Holiday said, 'what you did today; burying a friend.'

Savidge took some time to reply. Then: 'That was bad enough but it's more than that. I been thinking about the manner of his killing. It's struck me that if I hadn't intervened, he might be alive today.'

'Don't blame yourself for anything, Joe. Whether they killed him intentionally, or by accident, *they* were the cause of the whole situation, don't forget that.'

'Maybe my sticking my nose in was the trigger for the situation to get out of hand. My intention was to give him the opportunity to get away. But maybe when I was knocked down Flying Dog turned back to help me.'

'You said he was shot in the back. That means he had his back to them and was leaving.'

70

'Thanks for trying to give me some comfort, but it doesn't necessarily follow. He may have come back to me when he saw me go down and was kneeling down beside me with his back to them when they shot him.' He looked down at the tablecloth and sighed noisily. 'I don't know the precise facts. Suppose I'll never know. But if that's what happened, then I was the cause of his getting killed.'

'You have no reason to blame yourself.'

'I don't know exactly how he died. I was knocked unconscious and when I came to I was in the back of a wagon on the way to Pioche. Flying Dog was shot all right — in the back. I could see that from the body I buried. But I don't know exactly how it happened. Who did I think I was anyway? Butting in like some fool Sir Galahad.'

'From what you've told me the gang were out for trouble. And whatever the result, it was their fault, not yours. Doesn't matter which of them pulled the trigger. One did it and the others condoned it.'

He cast his mind back. 'There were three in the gang causing the trouble. Could have been any of them: Gelder, an old guy; Link Turner, a tough hotheaded kid; and their boss Leo Fage. But I don't know which of them actually did it. Probably was the younker. He was the one throwing the lead for the fun of it. But the last I saw of Gelder, he had a Winchester in his hands. However it happened, Fage was obviously party to it because it was he who paid the wagoner to get rid of the evidence.'

She reacted visibly to what he had just said. 'So it was the Fage bunch, eh? You think your friend was the first man they killed?'

'What do you mean? What do you know about it?'

'A couple of seconds back was the first time you've mentioned actual names. If you'd have told me the names earlier I would have understood the picture all the sooner.'

'What does that mean?'

'Awareness of the grip that the Fage bunch has over Bullionville is common knowledge even here in Pioche. Along with rumours of their willingness to gun down anybody who stands up to them.'

'I didn't know that. But I had cottoned to the fact that the local peace officer was prone to leave them be.'

'You were a newcomer to town: you would have found out how bad they were sooner or later.'

'Looks like I've found out about them too late — the hard way.'

'So — stop blaming yourself.'

★ ★ ★

Anton Valeur finished shaving. He dabbed the remnants of lather from his face, checked the results in the mirror, then rinsed the brush. He wiped the blade and put it, along with the shaving soap and brush, into their relevant

73

compartments in a small leather case. He sealed the container and placed it in his large travel-case, which was already packed with most of his belongings.

He donned his smart jacket, inspected its set in the mirror and took out his pocket watch, noting the o'clock. His passage on the noon stage to Mesquite was already booked giving ample time for him to take a leisurely breakfast.

He went downstairs and took up his usual seat in the hotel dining room. From the window he could see a clutch of cedars, the prevalence of which had led to Cedar City getting its name when first settled by Mormons — only trouble being the trees were junipers wrongly named. Not that he, the Mormons or anyone else was bothered.

He was sipping his coffee when a uniformed man presented himself at the table. 'Telegraph for Mr Valeur,' the man said, handing the diner a piece of paper.

The Frenchman read it. There was a beam on his face as he re-read the message.

'Will there be a reply, sir?' the telegraphist eventually asked.

'When is the coach to Pioche due out?'

The man glanced at the large clock against the wall. 'In about half an hour, sir.'

'*Très commode*,' the seated man said. 'There will be a reply.'

The official took out his pad in readiness. 'Yes, sir?'

'To be addressed to the sender as given on the original message: Miss Holiday Smith, The Overlander, Pioche. Message to read: Thank you. Will arrive on next stage.'

The official wrote down the words and read them back aloud.

'Keep the change,' the diner said, handing the man a bill.

'Thank you, sir. The message will be sent immediately.'

When the man had disappeared, Valeur dabbed his lips with the napkin and lit a panatella. After a moment's satisfied contemplation, he headed out and minutes later he was in the stage-line's booking office.

'I am booked on the noon stage out to Mesquite,' he said, 'but there has been a change in my requirements. Can I transfer to the next coach out to Pioche?'

'Certainly, sir.'

'Due out soon, I gather.'

The man checked his watch. 'Yes, sir. Within the quarter-hour.'

* * *

Two men were playing checkers on the boardwalk outside a store that proclaimed itself to be The Cedar City Mercantile.

One was a short, stocky fellow with a podgy, pockmarked face. As he studied the squared board he rubbed his suet-pudding features. 'Think you've got me, don't you, Mr Trane?' he said after a while. He finally moved a piece and added, 'But you ain't.'

The other was tall, with long greasy

hair down to his shoulders. He gazed at the new layout with almost colourless eyes, his pale features suggesting he was an indoor man. 'I'm afraid, my dear Mr Berens, that you walked into the trap.'

The short man watched helplessly as his companion hopped his black men around the board. He grunted when he saw the last of his whites being removed. 'One day I'm gonna learn how to play this damn game,' he said.

'I've told you,' his companion said, 'first time you beat me, we play for money — serious money.'

The winner stood up and peered at the clock through the grimy window of the store behind him. 'Nearly time,' he said. 'Let's get the horses.'

His companion folded up the board and dropped it into a bag together with the checkers. Then the two men walked a block to the stable to take possession of their mounts.

'One of your horses is throwing a shoe,' the stableman said when they showed up.

'Which one?' the tall one asked.

'The bay,' the stableman said, patting the rump of the relevant animal. 'Off-hind foot.'

'Hell! We're aiming to leave town as of now — pronto.'

'Won't take long,' the ostler said. He got behind the horse and expertly raised the leg to show a split shoe. 'But it needs seeing to, look. Don't matter how pronto you wanna leave town, you go far with it in this state and you'll have a lame horse come half an hour. Then you won't be going anywheres on it.'

'Exactly how long will it take to fix?' the tall one asked impatiently.

'Twenty minutes at the most, Mr Trane.'

'OK,' the tall man said. 'See to it. And make it quick.' He took his companion to the door. 'I'll stay here while the job gets done. You get back to the main drag and watch for the coach.'

He returned and drummed his fingers on the top of a stall rail as he watched the ostler take a handful of shoes from the wall.

'You're in luck,' the stableman said, as he set about his task. 'I always keep some readymade shoes in stock.'

He raised the hind leg and clenched it between his knees. Testing each shoe against the hoof he picked the one that was the closest fit. He removed the worn-down shoe and began paring back the horn of the foot.

Some quarter of an hour later he had hammered the new shoe into a tight fit and was now trimming the result with a heavy rasp.

The tall one was looking impatiently at his pocket watch when his companion came to the door and beckoned him.

'He didn't get on the Mesquite stage, boss,' he whispered.

'What? The stage left without him?'

'Yeah.'

'You sure?'

'Had a good look at every passenger who got on. He wasn't among them.'

When the shoe-fitting was over, the tall one paid the ostler and the twosome led their horses round to the main drag and tethered them to a hitch rail.

'Stay here,' Trane said.

He walked over to the stage office.

'Where's the other guy who's usually behind the desk?' he asked of the clerk. 'He was supposed to pass on some information to me.'

'He got called away unexpectedly, sir. His wife had gone into labour.'

Trane grunted. The fewer people who knew of his business the more he liked it. He accepted the fact that disclosing some of his intention wasn't to be avoided.

He leant over the counter. 'A certain Anton Valeur was figuring to leave on the Mesquite stage and your colleague was supposed to tell me if the gent made a change in his plans.'

'I don't know about that, sir. But I can say I was on duty when Mr Valeur changed his booking.'

'And?'

'He switched his booking to the Pioche coach.'

'When does that leave?'

'It went early this morning, sir.'

The tall man cursed and left the office without another word.

'We're riding on to Pioche,' he said to his companion when he rejoined him beside the horses. 'That's where the guy is now headed. God knows why. He's been there already.'

* * *

Having rested for another day, Savidge was feeling yards better and was sitting outside The Overlander taking in the sun. Throughout his periods of rest he had been thinking over his situation. Some time he was going to make the journey all the way back to Bullionville. There were three bastards back there that had a debt to pay and the way he saw it he was the only one around to enforce payment; just as he'd been the only one to lay the old man beneath the sod with any semblance of dignity. But to get to Bullionville he needed his own horse. And to do what he had to do when he got there he needed a brace of guns on his hips. Good guns he could rely on. But a horse and weaponry required money.

Somehow he had to get the wherewithal. Maybe working for a spell. Pioche was another mining town, work which he could handle. But first he needed a well body, and that called for more rest, which is why he was satisfied in the meantime to take in the sun on The Overlander veranda as the guest of a certain Miss Holiday Smith.

He watched the daily six-horse Concorde trundle by. Once it had come to a halt in the middle of town, he paid it no mind and so didn't see the passengers disembark.

One of them, baggage in hand, made his way back up the drag and stopped outside The Overlander. As the man cast his eyes up and down the edifice, Savidge appraised him. Smartly dressed, the man looked out of place in a scruffy mining town like Pioche. And, when he spoke, his voice demonstrated another difference.

'Excuse me, *m'sieur*,' he said in a strong foreign accent. 'Is Miss Holiday Smith at home?'

Savidge rose and opened the door. 'Holiday! You got company!'

'Coming,' came a distant voice.

He gestured for the visitor to enter and then followed him inside.

'Anton!' Holiday said by way of greeting, as she made her way down the stairs. 'How good to see you again!'

The Frenchman raised his arms. 'Ah, Holiday, *mon petit chou*, as charming as ever.'

Savidge had no claims on this woman but he felt unexplained pangs of jealousy at the expressions of affection between the two. He dropped into a seat out of the way. This was nothing to do with him. And what the hell was a *petit chou*?

The couple embraced, kissed each

83

other on cheeks, and exchanged more pleasantries. All to Savidge's increasing discomfort.

Then Holiday broke away and gestured to the seated man. 'This is Joe Savidge, a guest. And, Joe, this is Anton Valeur, an old friend.'

The two men exchanged nods.

'I can't believe how quickly it's taken you to get here,' Holiday went on.

'By chance I had not moved on, and so I was still lodged in Cedar City. It was heartening to receive your wire. Just before I was due to leave, in fact.'

Then the Frenchman threw a short glance in Savidge's direction. He turned back to Holiday and said quietly, 'Is there some place we can talk — privately?'

'Of course,' Holiday said and escorted the visitor to a side room.

Savidge watched them disappear behind a closed door. He was liking this fellow less by the minute. He grunted to himself and returned to his seat outside in the sun.

8

'It was so good of you to remember and even contact me,' the Frenchman said to Holiday after some more pleasantries. 'You have the artefacts?'

'The coins?'

'*Oui, mam'selle*. The coins.'

She took them from a drawer and gave them to him.

He took them to the light of a window. '*Magnifique*! Superb examples. Even better than I'd been hoping for! Tangible evidence.'

'Evidence of what?'

'That my countrymen were out this far west. As I told you, I'm writing a book on the French experience in your country. We know of their settling in Canada and Louisiana obviously, but that seems to be the limit of our knowledge of their travels. You acquired them from a local source?'

'Yes.' She laughed. 'Playing cards would you believe? Poker — just like you and I played. Remember?'

'Indeed, I do, *mam'selle*. That brings back happy memories. We enjoyed a few good games, did we not?'

'But I'm still at a loss as to what these things prove. This far west we get all kinds of currencies. A few French coins don't prove anything.'

'Of course, they don't. You are quite right. But they could indicate that my countrymen have been out here at least. How much will you take for them?'

She laughed. 'Nothing. At the poker table we used them as five-dollar tokens but they are yours for nothing. They obviously mean more to you than me.'

'*Merci, mam'selle*,' he said and kissed her. 'Monetarily they may not be worth much. I guess five dollars would be about right. But their real value lies in what they can tell us about history.' He weighed the coins in his hand. 'This game in which you won them, was it here in town?'

86

'Yes. The Golden Nugget saloon a few blocks down.'

'And the man from whom you acquired them, he is local? Not some stranger passing through?'

'He's an old-timer. Now, what's his name?' She threw her mind back. 'Jed, that's it. And I've seen him often enough around town to figure he must be a local gent.'

The man patted his hands in apparent triumph. 'This is getting better. Could you take me to him?'

'Don't know where he lives, but shouldn't be too much trouble to find out.'

★　★　★

It took half an hour of enquiries but eventually they located the place: lodgings at the end of town.

The landlady was dressed in dark colours with her hair gathered into a neat bun at the back of her head. Religious icons decorated the walls. She

87

frowned when the couple presented themselves. 'I'm afraid the poor man's not available for visitors. God has ordained that he is not to be well, poor soul that he is. He has to be kept as quiet as possible, the doctor says.'

'We'll be quiet,' Holiday said.

'It's not just that. The doctor was explicit about him not being disturbed.'

'What's the matter with him?'

'Went down with something. Doctor can't tell what. Says it's just old age catching up with him at long last.'

'Jed knows me,' Holiday said. 'I don't think that he'd mind me visiting him.'

The woman scowled. 'Everybody in town knows you, Miss Smith. You and your establishment! Don't mean a thing, him saying he knows you.'

'He's not been to my establishment. We know each other through convivial evenings in The Golden Nugget.'

'Drinking and playing cards!' the woman exclaimed, looking at a picture of the Virgin on the wall then crossing herself. 'Almost as bad.'

She tutted. 'He's struggled to pay his rent for as long as he's been here. Losing most of what he gets through drink and games of chance. The only reason why I've put up with him for so long is he's had nowhere else to go.' She sniffed. 'We are taught to be charitable.'

Holiday could see she was getting nowhere and needed to try another tack. She gestured to her companion. 'My friend here has travelled a long way to see him.

'That is true, *madame*,' Valeur said. 'A very long way.'

'I'm sure Jed wouldn't turn him away,' Holiday added.

The woman looked unaffected by the information.

'I have come all the way from La France, *madame*,' Valeur said.

The woman studied the Frenchman. At least he looked respectable. And, after all, the French were Catholic.

She pondered. 'France? That *is* a long way. Very well. Follow me. But only for a short time and you must be quiet. No excitement.'

She led them upstairs and gingerly knocked at a door. 'You got visitors, Jed. Are you available and decent?'

'Sure,' came a weak voice. 'Be glad of some company.'

They pulled up chairs and, when the landlady had gone, the Frenchman took out the coins. 'You recognize these historical relics that were won from you in a card game by this lady, Holiday Smith?'

'Yes, sir.'

'How did you acquire these particular items of currency?'

'I didn't steal them! Don't think that!'

Valeur smiled. 'I'm sure you didn't, *m'sieur*. And do not worry. I'm not a lawman and had no proprietorial rights in them before they came into your possession. The fact is, I'm trying to trace the past travels of my countrymen.' He passed one of the coins over to the old man. 'They're French, you see. Very old.'

The old man squinted at it and handed it back. 'French, eh? Hell, I couldn't even read the lettering on 'em. Just knew they looked like they were made of gold.'

'There may be some gold in them, depending on the date of issue. But only a negligible amount.'

'Only a negligible amount? Well, they were good enough to be accepted by Holiday here as a bet. And she won 'em fair and square. Good player.' He tried to wink in a conspiratorial way but the effort only resulted in a weak fluttering of his eye. 'Be wary if you ever play her, Mr Frenchie.' And he tried a wink again.

'I know. I have played her. So where did you originally get them? In another card game?'

'No. I found 'em.'

Valeur's eyebrows rose. 'Where?'

'Vegas Wells.'

The Frenchman looked at Holiday. She shook her head. 'Means nothing to me. Can't say I've ever heard of it.'

'Not many people have,' the old man chuckled. 'You only need to know where it is if you're stuck in the middle of nowhere and need water.'

'Can you take me to this — Vegas Wells?'

The old man coughed. 'I have trouble getting out of bed to use the pisspot these days, never mind trekking through the desert.' He pulled a hangdog expression in Holiday's direction. 'Oh, excuse my language, ma'am.'

'Don't worry about it, sir,' she said with a smile. 'I've heard far worse.'

'The desert?' Valeur persisted.

'Yeah. The Wells, it's a water-hole several days' trek into God's Hell Hole.' He chuckled and touched his nose. 'Only the Indians and a few old desert travellers like me know its whereat. But it's still got water.'

'What were the circumstances?'

The old man looked blank.

'Precisely how did you come across the coins?' Holiday explained.

'Last time I was prospecting out that

way. Prospecting, huh! Took me a lifetime to realize that prospecting ain't the way to making my fortune. Anyways, turned up nothing as usual and, before heading back, I made for the Wells to get water before setting out on my return journey through the desert.'

'This place — this Vegas Wells — how big is it?'

'Just a few derelict buildings; lots of stuff travellers have dumped over the years. And water, of course — that's the important thing about the place.'

'And whereabouts exactly in this Vegas Wells did you find them?'

The old man thought about it. 'Near what could have been an orchard; something like that.'

'Orchard? What orchard?'

'I just use that name cos that's what it looks like — an orchard. But there's no fruit or nothing growing there now, just a few dried-up stumps. See, over the centuries a lot of folk have been there. Spanish used it as a watering

93

place. Desert Injuns have used it as a base from time to time. Folks lost on the way west have found sustenance there. Think even the Mormons stopped by there once. But it's been deserted as long as folks can remember. I found the coins near the remains of what looked like it had been this orchard place. Anyways that's where I found your coins. Just stumbled across 'em.'

'Did you have to dig for them?'

'No. They were on the surface. Almost didn't see 'em, they were covered with so much sand and dust. It was the symmetrical shape that first caught my eye.'

'Did your discovery prompt you to search further?'

'Searched the ground in the area but didn't come up with anything. See, there's lots of signs that people have been there over the years. Buttons, old tools and of course, bits of skeletons, animal and human. So finding a couple of coins ain't nothing special.'

'There's nothing else you can tell me?'

The man shook his head weakly and closed his eyes.

Valeur touched the man's shoulder. 'You've been very helpful, sir, and I thank you for seeing us. Is there anything I can do for you?'

The old man chuckled feebly. 'Not unless you got a bottle of whiskey tucked away in your pocket.'

'I haven't, but I'll get one for you. And I hope you get better quickly, *m'sieur*.'

The landlady was waiting at the bottom of the stairs.

'What exactly is the matter with him, *madame*?' Valeur asked, before they made their goodbyes.

'Doctor's not sure. With old people you can never tell. The slightest thing can set them on a downward path. Nobody knows how old the feller is, but Doctor thinks he's had his full score and ten and the end can't be far off. Simple as that.'

Outside, Valeur looked up and down the street. 'So he's not going to be able to take me out there.'

'Why the need to go?' Holiday asked.

'The fellow talked of several people coming across it over time. Amongst those there could have been some French trekkers. Maybe it had been a French settlement for a period. Such a discovery would be an important link in drafting the history of French settlers in these parts. There might be more evidence of that out there in the desert. I can't wait to cable the institute in Paris.'

'Now, if I were you, Anton, I'd put a hold on sending cables and such. Fact is, it looks to me like grasping at straws. At least at the moment.'

His face was expressionless, as though he hadn't heard her. 'Do you know of anyone who could act as a guide for me?'

She shook her head. 'You heard old Jed. Only prospectors and Indians know its whereabouts. Pioche's just made up of miners. The mining companies have tapped all the lodes in these parts. No need for prospectors any more. They all moved on years back, responding to the call of precious metal in more remote regions. Save for old Jed. He's the only prospector left and there are no Indians in town.'

'After I've taken the old feller his liquor, I'll make enquiries.'

★   ★   ★

An hour later Valeur returned to The Overlander where Holiday was preparing a meal. He'd taken the promised bottle to the old prospector, smuggling it past the suspicious landlady, then toured the saloons investigating the prospect of employing a guide.

'You're right,' he said as he joined her in the kitchen. 'Mining is the only thing anybody knows about round here.'

'Don't give up yet,' she said, wiping her hands. 'I've got an idea. Come with me.'

Outside they passed Savidge who was sitting on the veranda.

'I'm going out for a few minutes, Joe,' she said. 'Can you keep your eye on the pots on the stove?'

'Sure.'

'Sam Hedley is the town butcher,' Holiday explained, as the two walked along the boardwalk. 'Been here since the beginning. Town was a couple of shacks then. What he doesn't know about folk in town ain't worth a red cent. If there's a man within twenty miles who's acquainted with the desert, Sam will be able to point a knowledge-able finger at him.'

9

A quarter of an hour on the couple were walking back to The Overlander.

'I'm sorry,' Holiday was saying, 'but if Sam doesn't know of anyone, then believe me, there isn't anyone.' The reliable butcher who knew everybody in town had drawn a blank.

'Well, thanks for trying, *ma chérie*,' the Frenchman said. 'But I am not disheartened, for this is just the beginning. If there's no one here who can help I'll catch the coach tomorrow and try another town. We're so close to the desert there must be someone in the region who knows their way across it and how to get to this mysterious Vegas Wells.'

'I don't want to dampen your spirits,' she said, as she opened the door, 'but the desert is an inhospitable wilderness with nothing to offer. As a betting woman I wouldn't give odds on you finding anyone.'

Savidge was stabbing a knife into potatoes in a steaming pot when they entered the kitchen.

''Bout time,' Savidge said. 'Any longer and these spuds would have been pure mush.'

He transferred steaks from the grill to the plates already set out on the table while Holiday set about topping them up with vegetables.

'Been a long time since I sweated over a stove,' Savidge said, as they settled down to their meal.

'Don't hurt for a male of the species to have a hand in household chores,' Holiday said.

'If he has to,' Savidge grunted. 'As long as he doesn't make a habit of it.'

'The man, he cooks a lot in France,' Valeur said. 'In our country we don't believe in leaving all such things to the lady of the house.'

'Seems to me,' Holiday said, raising a fork in emphasis, 'that France is a more civilized country in many ways.'

'Don't know about that,' Savidge said. 'Never been.'

'Well, whoever cooked this,' Valeur said, 'man or woman, it is splendid fare.'

'Thank you,' Holiday said.

The conversation ebbed until the main course was over and Holiday proclaimed, 'And now for the *pièce de résistance!*'

She laid out three bowls, fetched the same number of cans from a cupboard and handed Savidge a can-opener. 'One of my weaknesses,' she said. 'Canned peaches. Something of a luxury out here.' She scoured the cupboard adding, 'Which reminds me I'm out of stock again. Must get some more.'

When they had finished their desserts Savidge said, 'You two have had a busy morning by all appearances.'

'But an unfruitful one,' Valeur said.

'Our visitor wishes to go into the desert, Joe,' Holiday explained, 'but he cannot find a guide.'

Savidge frowned. 'In a place like this you cannot find someone who knows the desert? It's only a spit and a holler away.'

'That is the case, *m'sieur*. The town is full of men who know everything there is to know about extracting ore from the ground and tradesmen who cater to the miners' every need but there is no one who is familiar with local geography! *Incroyable*!'

'Why do you wish to go into the desert?' Savidge asked. 'There's nothing there.'

'M'sieur Valeur is an historian,' Holiday explained.

'Associated with The Lycée in Paris,' the Frenchman elaborated. 'You have heard of it, *m'sieur*?'

Savidge shook his head. 'Don't even know what it is.'

'It is a famous place of study, *m'sieur*.'

'Anton is interested in the history of French settlers out here,' she went on.

Savidge's brow puckered. 'Well, I

haven't had much education so I don't know much. I heard of Germans settling on the High Plains in Texas. And the Spanish were the first colonists out here, of course, but never heard of French settlers this far west.'

'That is what is so intriguing,' Valeur said. 'It is not proven but it is a possibility.'

'M'sieur Valeur is writing a book on these things,' she said by way of elaboration.

'Not much of a reader myself,' Savidge said, 'but I did read a book once.'

'Oh yes?' Holiday said. 'What was it about?'

'Can't remember. But it was a big red one.'

She looked askance until she caught his smile.

'So where exactly do you want to go?' Savidge continued.

'A lost place called Vegas Wells,' the Frenchman said.

'It ain't so lost,' Savidge said.

'What do you mean?' Valeur asked.

'When white men say a place is 'lost' they simply mean it's not locatable by the white man. In the same way down in South America they talk of lost cities in the jungle but the Indians out there know of the places and exactly where they are. So they are not really 'lost'.'

Valeur nodded. 'Yes, I see what you mean. And this is the way that Vegas Wells is a 'lost' settlement?'

'You've hit it, Anton.' Then, 'Why do you want to go out there?'

'He's traced some coins that came from the place,' Holiday explained.

'Coins,' Valeur echoed. 'But as an historian, I prefer the word artefacts.'

★   ★   ★

When they had finished the meal, Savidge said, 'We males shall wash the dishes. Right, Anton? That way we can class ourselves as being civilized.' And he winked at Holiday.

Later, when the chore was over, the

three were reclining in the lobby. Valeur offered panatellas to his companions and they smoked reflectively.

'So Vegas Wells is *not* a lost settlement you say, Joe,' Valeur said.

'Don't figure it is.'

'Well, who would know where it is? We have learned that only Indians and a few prospectors have any idea of its whereabouts.'

Savidge smiled and watched the smoke from his panatella as it rose to the high ceiling of the lobby. Eventually he said, '*I* know.'

Surprise registered in the Frenchman's features. 'You, *m'sieur?*'

Savidge nodded. 'Ain't an easy place to get to — and that's a fact — but with water and supplies, it's possible.'

Valeur studied the man's features to see if he was joking. 'You sound like you know what you're talking about.'

Savidge nodded again. 'Figure so. I guess being Nevada-born and bred means I do know what I'm talking about.'

'Tell me more.'

'I'll tell you one thing — it's too hazardous to attempt getting to the place unless one's got a damn good reason.'

'I have a damn good reason.'

The word 'damn' sounded out of place coming from the Frenchman's mouth.

'How damn good?'

'I'm willing to pay.'

Savidge drew on his cigar and touched its ash into an ashtray. 'How does that willingness translate into US currency?'

'Let me get this straight — are you offering your services as a guide?'

'Depends on what it pays.'

'How much would you want?'

Savidge ruminated on the grim task he had scheduled for himself back in Bullionville. 'For a start, enough to buy a horse and guns. Reckon five hundred dollars would cover it.'

The Frenchman grimaced. 'Five hundred? That's quite a sum. And certainly a lot of money for the things you say you want to buy with it.'

'I got things to do and for that I need a *good* horse and *quality* guns — the best. And something for my time, of course. Yeah, five hundred would do it, I figure.'

'If five hundred is what is needed for your services, *m'sieur*, then it is done.'

The Frenchman's ready acceptance of such a sum took Savidge aback. 'And you finance supplies and necessaries like mules?'

'Naturally, *m'sieur.*'

Savidge nodded.

The Frenchman looked at Holiday. 'Well, what do you know? After all our perambulations, *mam'selle*, the solution to my problem lay right here in the very Overlander itself! It has indeed been a good day's work. *D'accord*, when can we start, *m'sieur*?'

'How soon do you want to go?'

'As soon as possible.'

'OK, sun up tomorrow. That'll give us all afternoon to get supplies and to get kitted out — should be ample time.'

'Are you sure you're going to be OK,

Joe?' Holiday asked. 'Isn't tomorrow a little early for such a strenuous task? Couldn't you do with a little more rest?' She looked at the Frenchman. 'Joe is still recovering from a bad beating,' she added by way of explanation.

Valeur ignored her observation, his movements becoming energetic, demonstrating the single track in which his mind ran. 'For the journey, what do we need, *m'sieur*?'

Savidge thought on it. 'Before I start drawing up a list of requirements for the trip, *I* need half my fee up front. Cash.'

'I don't carry that much in currency,' the Frenchman said.

Savidge shrugged as though to say the deal was off and remained silent.

Valeur looked at the woman. 'But there's a good bank in town, is there not?'

She nodded.

'*D'accord*. I have the necessary identification for presentation at the bank. You can have the money this very afternoon, my dear Joe — if you so wish.'

'I so wish,' Savidge said, and looked at Holiday. 'You can hold the cash for me while I'm away?'

'You trust me?'

'Hellfire, Holiday, you've looked after me OK so far.'

'So what do we need?' Valeur continued.

'Two mules each. One to carry supplies and one for riding when terrain allows. Not the least of the problems is going to be the sun, so we need tents. It's going to be like being under a magnifying glass out there. So, one tent for us and a tarp or two that we can set up as an awning for the animals when the sun gets high. Plus, of course, eats for a week and as much water as the animals can carry. And some armoury, say a couple of carbines, for unseen circumstances.'

★ ★ ★

It was late afternoon. The two men had spent a long time trawling the stores

109

and were now in the backyard of The Overlander where Savidge was pointing at stacked items one by one and ticking them off on a grubby piece of paper: jerky, bread, coffee, oats, oranges.

He checked the saddles on two of the four large mules he had selected for Valeur to purchase. 'They say camels are best for desert travel but, in their absence, mules are hardier than most horses. It's no tale that they can be obstinate but these are well broke.'

He walked among the animals, patting them and talking soothingly. 'Before you hit the sack tonight, Anton, spend some time with them so they get to know your voice and smell. That way they won't see you as a threat when we come to use them.'

Finally he checked their bridles, then searched through the stacks and took out some empty bags. He called for scissors from Holiday and proceeded to trim the bags. Then one by one, and with great difficulty, he fitted the adapted bags to the bridles so that most of the animal's head was covered. All the time he reassured them by patting and talking quietly.

Valeur looked at the now blind, agitated mules. 'Why have you bagged their heads, *m'sieur*? They will not be able to see where they are going. Surely that will make them more disturbed?'

'Have a look at how I've fixed them. You might have to do it fast in an emergency. There can be bad sand storms out there. You and I can cover our eyes: they can't — and the last thing we want fifty miles from nowhere is blinded mokes.'

★ ★ ★

The clock in the lobby had chimed midnight long past. Everything was ready for an early morning start and the two men, together with Holiday, were taking last minute smokes on the frontage of The Overlander.

'I will wish you both *bonne nuit*,' Valeur said, flicking the butt of his panatela into the drag and yawning. 'I need some sleep.'

'Are you sure you'll be up to it tomorrow?' Holiday asked Savidge when the Frenchman had disappeared inside.

'As good as I'm gonna be.'

There was a pause. Moths fluttered noisily round the lighted glass and cicadas clicked in the darkness.

'I'm gonna miss you,' Holiday said after a while.

Savidge cleared his throat in an attempt to cover his discomfiture at such an expression of sentiment. 'We've only known each other a couple of days.'

'One thing I'm learning late in life, Joe, is that it seems' — she paused while she searched for the right word — 'that fondness doesn't depend on how long you've known a person.'

Unsure of how to handle the situation, Savidge reached out his hand for hers. 'You've been good to me, Holiday. Ain't no gainsaying that, looking after me and all. You're a very special woman.'

They stayed that way for some time. Eventually he gave her hand a squeeze and let it go, saying, 'Don't worry about me, Holiday. I'm gonna be back. You can put money on that.'

'What are you gonna do when you get back?'

'Some loose ends in Bullionville need attending to.'

'Oh,' she said softly with a hint of disappointment in her voice. 'And after that?'

'Ain't thought that far ahead.'

10

The first leg of their journey took in the Old Spanish Trail. For a long time the two men headed along the well-rutted roads passing settlers in their covered wagons and Eastern tradesman hauling their goods to California. They rode through sand and dust churned up by herds of California-bred horses bound for Missouri.

The further west they travelled the more inhospitable became the country with nothing but semi-desert terrain on either side of the trail, windswept sand blurring into the distance.

Mid-afternoon on the second day Savidge reined in. Furry with dust and sweat, he wiped his brow, then pointed north beyond the trail. 'This is where we turn off the trail and head into the desert. From now on it really starts to get tough.'

His companion looked at the terrain: a smooth, unbroken layer of windswept sand, a seemingly unending stretch of aridness, a hole in the map.

'Reckon you think it looks bad,' Savidge said, gazing across the scrubby, dry plain, 'Hot and dry. But lack of water will not be a problem for a spell. Nevertheless we should still be sparing with it just in case.' He pointed to a small bunch of lonely trees some distance into the desert. 'We'll rest over there for a few hours. We'll take advantage of trees while we can. Shade yourself and try to get some sleep and we'll continue when the sun has dropped a piece.'

By the time they'd rested and caught snatches of elusive sleep, the sun had fallen.

'I know it doesn't seem that way,' Savidge said, as he pulled his gear together, 'but it is getting cooler, which is what we need for travel.'

And they headed into the sands.

At first the going wasn't too bad.

The ground was hard-packed in most places, enabling hoofs to get a grip so that the men could stay in the saddle. But soon their eyes smarted with the salt sting of sweat. From time to time Savidge would catch sight of some small pool. He knew the signs. The sand would be a different colour and there would be touches of green around the edges. The water was brackish but enough for the needs of their mules and themselves.

Once they had sated themselves at such oases they refilled canteens, then splashed the stuff over themselves and animals before pushing on.

Shadows had lengthened further and for the first time they sensed the drop in temperature.

'Should we not bivouac now?' Valeur asked. 'I'm bushed.'

Savidge laughed. 'We've only just started. OK, we'll take a break, have a bite. But we'll only make it a short spell. I know we're both tired but conditions are going to get a lot worse than this and we've got to prepare for them. The first rule of prolonged desert journeying is to hole up during the day, restricting travel to night and cooler hours.'

'But I'm ready to drop now,' Valeur said.

'You knew it was not going to be a picnic,' the other said. 'We've got several more days of hard slog to go yet. And it gets worse. Best we get into the rhythm now while we can.'

An hour on, after a brief meal and rest up, they pushed out again across the darkening bleak tableland. As the heat lessened, the other problem, that of tiredness began to predominate.

Eventually the sand became too soft for them to ride and they dismounted and proceeded on foot. But Savidge eventually called a final halt when they could hardly see where to place their feet, rendering safe passage near impossible.

★ ★ ★

At the first sign of light they resumed they trek, only stopping when the sun became a blistering fester once more. They set up the tent and awning for the animals.

'I'm low on water,' Valeur said.

Savidge shook the Frenchman's canteen. 'You got a few mouthfuls there, Anton. A sip when necessary will be enough to see you through to the next source of water.'

And they bedded down, accepting sleep if it chose to come.

* * *

The sun was rising fast during their next travelling session when Savidge halted with the words, 'We'll take a break. Something needs attending to.'

'Shall I get the tents out?'

'No. We'll make this a short stop.' Savidge shaded his eyes and looked ahead. 'We should be able to get another mile or so under our belt before the sun eventually makes our progress impossible again.'

He walked back to the end mule and checked its legs. 'We need to redistribute loads. I've noticed this one's developing a limp. May as well make the changes now. I'll use this one as a saddle horse when conditions allow.'

He patted its rump. 'Undo his rope while I unsaddle mine.'

'*Oui, m'sieur.*'

Savidge had just laid his saddle on the sand when there came a shout from Valeur. Savidge turned to see the mule that had been in the Frenchman's charge was now bolting along their backtrail.

'He just wrenched free!' Valeur shouted. 'I couldn't hold him.'

Savidge securely tethered the remaining three to a dead stump, then looked back. 'Hell! That's the one with the tents.'

Instinctively he loped a few paces but soon stopped. 'I'll never catch him. He's clear got it into his head that things are better back that-aways. Can't blame him. He's right on that score.

Our only hope is that he returns to us of his own accord. We'll wait and see; and take the opportunity to slake our thirst and rest.'

But half an hour on, there was no sign of the recalcitrant animal.

'We'll not see him again,' Savidge concluded, as he peered into the horizon. He thought about the new development then turned to his companion. 'Nothing for it, my friend, but to turn back ourselves. Those tents were essential for survival out here. Trying to exist in the hellhole ahead without cover would be a crazy option.' He cursed, then muttered, 'Partly my fault. I shouldn't have put all the tents and tarps on the same animal. A greenhorn mistake if ever there was one.'

'We cannot go back, *m'sieur*!'

'Listen. We've nowhere near broken the back of our journey. Continuing simply isn't on, pal. Not without cover. Worse, the renegade moke was carrying a goodly amount of our water supply.'

'Can we not seek shade with trees

and cacti, like we've done before?'

Savidge pointed to the bleakness ahead. 'Use your eyes. What trees? And what cacti there are will not provide enough shade when it gets real bad.'

'We cannot give up so early on, m'sieur.'

Savidge said nothing.

Then the Frenchman said, 'May I remind you I have paid you half your fee. That means I trust you.'

Savidge thought on it. He felt cornered by the Frenchman's words. 'OK, tell you what — we'll continue for the time being,' he concluded, in the face of the verbal blackmail. Then he gestured at the sun. 'But if it gets real bad, sun-wise or water-wise, we turn back on my say-so — with no argument. Agreed?'

'Agreed.'

★   ★   ★

Their next rest-up was taken when they came across a bunch of cacti, small but large enough to provide them with a little shade.

Valeur opened his eyes after a nap. The remaining mules, still roped together but otherwise free, were gathered some hundred yards away, busily occupied in some activity.

'What they doing?' he asked.

Savidge grinned. 'They've found some moisture. I let them loose while we were resting. Kept my eye on them. I knew I could rely on them.'

'Weren't you afraid they would scoot like the other beast?'

Savidge shook his head. 'No. I could tell he was the maverick of the bunch. Besides they're roped together. Like that they think they're still in our charge. Wouldn't occur to them to vamoose. They're bright but not that bright.'

He rose and staggered towards the animals. He dropped to his knees to ladle up some of the precious liquid from the source that the animals had instinctively located.

The Frenchman joined him. 'There's barely an inch of water,' he said, dropping to his knees.

Savidge grinned again. 'Don't fret, my dear Anton. Doesn't matter how much the mules take, or how much you drink, you'll observe that within seconds there's always an inch left. That's the way these things work. Just takes time is all.'

With their remaining canteens once more replenished and the burning globe of the sun beginning to drop they resumed their journey.

11

After another rest-up while the desert had turned into an oven, they pressed on again. But, despite their being sparing in use of water, it wasn't long before the canteens were dangerously low once more.

'When are we going to find some more water?' the Frenchman croaked, his tongue running over cracked lips. 'I don't think I can last much longer.'

'Yes, you can,' Savidge said, smiling.

'What the hell you got to smile at?' Valeur snapped, his veneer of politeness cracking for the first time.

The other paused and raised a finger.

'What you doing?' the exasperated Frenchman wanted to know.

'Listen. That's a quail. Can't you hear it? It's faint but it's a quail all right.'

'This is hell of a time to be bird

fancier,' Valeur grunted. 'And I cannot hear anything.'

'And haven't you heard the occasional coyote howl? Each one a little louder.'

'I think the sun's turning you loopy, *m'sieur*. I have heard nothing but the sound of my feet crunching sun-baked ground.'

'Listen and learn, my friend. You can gain comfort from the sound of animal life. It should give you some assurance that we're not alone in this alien world. They're evidence of life and, more important, that means that water can't be too far away. They know where the stuff is, like the mules, which is why I been studying the ground for the minutest of tracks.' He pointed downward. 'Sign tells me we're almost there.'

Valeur scrutinized the ground. 'What sign? What are you, *m'sieur*, some kind of wizard? And how does a miner know these things?'

The guide smiled, ignoring the comment. Then, five minutes on, he stopped and inspected the ground more closely. He pointed to the side, away from their course. 'Just about there I would say.'

He moved across the cracked ground in the direction he had indicated. Valeur watched him drop to his knees. He followed and watched him scooping earth away from the middle of some dampness until there was a hole about a foot in depth. He looked up at his companion, smiled, slumped back and waited.

Wide-eyed, Valeur watched the dampness become clear moisture, and the moisture thicken to a distinct wetness. 'Yes, you are a damn wizard, *mon ami*.'

'In time there'll be enough for us to submerge and fill our canteens, and water the animals. And for a gentleman like yourself, maybe even enough for some civilized washing.'

After Valeur had put the top on his second full container, he hefted it. 'Gold, *m'sieur*. Pure gold.'

During the next period of darkness they were taking a meal when Savidge suddenly stiffened. Silently he looked one way then the other. He moved out of the firelight and peered into the distance along their backtrail.

'Figure we got company,' he whispered. 'Carry on with what you were doing like nothing was amiss.'

He bent double, pulled a carbine from its boot and loped into the darkness. He went round in a semi-circle, then lowered himself behind a dune and watched.

He had been right. There was a silhouetted figure moving towards their camp.

He continued to circle the terrain so that eventually he was to the rear of the mysterious shape. Whoever it was made no attempt to be furtive on approach to the camp-fire. Then he knew why. As he came up behind the figure a familiar scent wafted back to his nostrils. Heliotrope!

And he heard Valeur exclaim, 'Holiday!'

Savidge followed her to the camp. 'Nearly got your pretty head blowed off there, ma'am,' he said, lowering his gun.

'What brings you out here, *madame*?' Valeur asked in an almost polite tone.

'Water,' she gasped, 'water.'

Savidge took the top off his canteen and handed it to her.

'Thank you,' she said, clumsily upending the container so that water splattered her face and dripped from her chin.

'Careful.' Savidge said sternly. 'Don't waste it.' Then: 'And what the hell are you doing out here?' he added, in an equally stern tone.

'And how did you make it through the desert?' Valeur went on.

By then Savidge had got a good look at her in the light of the flames and he could see she was distraught. 'Hey, what's the matter, gal?'

'Looks like you're being followed,' she said.

'Yeah — by you,' Savidge replied harshly.

'No, by somebody other than me.' She pointed into the darkness of their backtrail. 'Back there.'

'How far back?'

'Couple of miles I figure. But it'll be less than that when they find I've managed to escape.'

'Managed to escape?' Valeur echoed.

Savidge suddenly pulled her to him, wrapped his arms around her. 'Gee, I'm sorry for sounding inhospitable, Holiday. I don't know what you've been through. It was just the thought of you being out here in this hellhole. It shocked me.'

He became aware of her beginning to sob.

'You crying, gal?'

'No, of course not.'

'The notion of you putting yourself at risk, that's what was concerning me,' he went on. 'But I reckon it wasn't your doing.' His arms still around her he walked her towards the fire. 'Come on, gal. Have a drink of coffee and calm

129

down. Then you can tell us all about it.'

As a tin mug was being filled for her she kept looking back. 'Couple of guys came to town asking questions. Something brought them to The Overlander and me. Don't know what. Said they were explorers. Told me they were out here to map as much of the desert as they could. I wanted to know what that had to do with me. They flannelled on but I could tell that their spiel was as false as a six-dollar bill.'

'What makes you say that?'

'For a start they seemed very interested in Anton and what he was doing.'

'Was there anything specific that they wanted to know?'

'They were very interested in the coins. Kept on about the historical significance of them. How important they could be in writing the history of the region. Talked about them just like Anton did. But the more time I've spent with them the more I felt it was all a cover.'

'And why are you with them out here?'

'They asked me to join them on their trek. I said no, of course. Why would I want to go into the desert? Next thing I knew — I was bound, gagged, kidnapped — and I was being brought into this Godforsaken place. Once we got moving it was obvious they were following your tracks. Don't know why.'

'And they're out there now, back a couple of miles?' Valeur pressed.

'Yeah. I figure they've been keeping their distance so that they don't arouse suspicion. But once they realize I've gone ahead and joined you, maybe they won't have a reason any more for keeping out of sight.'

'Wonder what the hell they're up to?' Savidge said.

He looked at the Frenchman who just gave a shrug, saying, 'Your guess is as good as mine, m'sieur.'

'And how come you made it here?' Savidge went on.

'Followed what I thought might be

the right direction after I managed to take off while we were all bedded down for the night.'

'These guys, can you describe them?'

'Well, there's two. A tall one who acts like the boss. And a short podgy-faced feller. One thing I do know, they don't look like explorers. Just ordinary guys.'

Savidge looked into the darkness. 'Something don't smell right. Best we start moving. And keep our eyes skinned on our backtrail.'

He began returning bits and pieces to the back of a mule. 'This trip was planned for two — not three — so from now on we gotta be extra careful with water and food.'

As he returned to the fire Holiday touched his arm. 'I'm sorry to be a burden, Joe. I just didn't know what to do.'

'From what you've told us about those guys, you did the right thing.' He put his hand on hers which was still resting on his arm. 'Cutting loose like that and trekking on by yourself was a very brave thing for you to do, gal.'

12

Everything began to feel heavy: belts, the boots dragging at feet. They were even conscious of the weight of their hats.

As the fireball rose in the sky, they felt their faces and necks turning raw red, the colour of the sand. The damn sand that looked as though it had been untouched for a thousand years. Out this far not a blade of grass or single tree had dared to push itself up through the flat red stuff or between the rock-holes.

They sorely recognized the need to rest, get out of the sun but there was no usable vegetation, the tallest of the sparse cacti little more than a couple of feet in height. All around them, sand which had never felt the touch of water was rippled as though by some long-gone invisible tide.

Rising dust choked, worked its way into crevices, their necks, eyes, ears. Their tongues were becoming hunks of wood in their mouths. Heads down, they tramped on, forcing leaden legs to move on.

★　★　★

The damn sun was relentless, bleeding its hot redness over everything. During the next stretch of their journey Valeur stumbled a couple of times and had to be helped to his feet by Savidge.

With the heat beating down through headgear, brains were on the verge of spinning.

Valeur particularly felt weak and sick. Time and time again he looked up and thought he could read death in the sun. 'How much further before we rest, Joe? I'm not doing too well here. I need shade.'

'Me, too,' Holiday groaned.

'I really think I'm gonna pass out,' Valeur added.

Savidge poured some precious fluid

on his kerchief and wiped the French-man's brow. 'Just try and hang on for a little longer. There's nothing in view that can afford shelter. If you pass out here under the sun, you'll get burnt to a crisp. And there's nothing we will be able to do about it.'

The Frenchman persevered, but some ten minutes on he muttered something about nature not endowing him with a constitution for these conditions, and he collapsed.

Savidge dropped down beside him and applied some more moisture to the man's face.

'Cover him with anything you can,' he said. 'I'll go on ahead and see what I can turn up.'

It wasn't long before he returned. 'There's a hollow. It's not the best but it will have to do. There are the stumps of long dead trees that'll afford as much shel-ter as we're likely to get out hereabouts.'

He hauled the semi-conscious French-man across the back of one of the mules and headed off. In the hollow he laid the man down. He could see the man was shaking.

'Think he's got a touch of desert fever,' he said.

'*Non*, not desert fever,' Valeur said weakly. 'Malaria. Get spasms every now and again. Got bitten once when serving in the colonies. The bout won't last long.' His eyes closed.

Savidge dampened his bandanna and applied it to the man's forehead but could tell by the way his head lolled that, despite the now violent shivering, he was out.

He lowered a saddle over him. The arch of it was just enough to get the unconscious man's head and part of his shoulder into shade. And he covered the remaining torso with a blanket.

'It'll get cooler soon,' Savidge said to Holiday. 'That should help him. Nothing for it but for us to camp here. Then we'll turn back. The man can't travel any further. It's only going to get hotter.'

He looked ahead into the distance.

'Pity, because by my reckoning we would have made Vegas Wells about noon tomorrow. I'll get a fire going and prepare some chow.' He trickled more water over his bandanna. 'Meantimes, you try to cool him down as much as you can. Who knows? A woman's touch might make all the difference.'

★   ★   ★

It was a couple of hours later. Savidge and Holiday had taken some food. The Frenchman was still sleeping. Savidge was lying on his back looking at the stars.

Holiday packed the platters she had been wiping and walked over to him. 'A penny for them.'

'For what?'

'Your thoughts.'

'Oh, I was just thinking what a mess we've gotten ourselves into.'

She dropped down and lay on her back beside him.

'So what are you thinking?' he asked.

'You'd never guess. Canned peaches! Would you believe it?'

'Well, one thing I can promise you, ma'am. You ain't gonna sample their delights for quite a few days yet.'

'Crazy, isn't it?' she continued. 'We're in dire need of water and decent food and all I can think of is canned peaches.'

'It's the desert. Plays tricks on the mind. Exaggerates the need for what you can't have.'

She snuggled against him. 'Romantic, isn't it, the night sky?'

'It's more than romantic, ma'am,' he said. 'Day and night, there's information up there. During the day you can get some idea of the time from the sun. And at night you can get a good estimate of where you are from the stars. Of course, you need instruments to work out exactly but, if you know them, they'll give a rough idea.'

'How is it a miner is so knowledgeable about such things?' she said. 'More specifically, how come you're so knowledgeable about the desert? I'd swear there are times when you seem to know every grain of sand. And your knowing the whereabouts of this Vegas Wells, a hundred miles into the depths of an uncharted hellhole. That came as a surprise. Especially when I learned that its location is supposedly only known to Indians and a few old prospectors. How come you know? A miner. What makes you so special, Mr Savidge?'

He didn't comment so she added, 'Well, I tell you one thing: you don't look like no old prospector to me.'

'Thanks for the compliment.'

'Well, I'm waiting.'

'Why the interrogation? We've survived so far. Ain't that enough?'

'This is not an interrogation,' the woman said. 'It's what's called after-dinner conversation. Otherwise known as polite chit chat.'

Savidge shrugged. 'There you go with your politeness and civilization thing again. OK, you want some polite chit-chat. No harm in your knowing. Fact is, I'm half Indian.'

Holiday's jaw dropped and she edged herself up onto her elbow so that she could inspect him more clearly.

Savidge smiled. 'Yeah, half Paiute. Look a little more intently at my features and you'll see my inheritance. The relatively fair skin and blue eyes are from my mother.' She leaned across and ran her fingers over his cheek.

'The high cheekbones and straight nose,' he went on, 'those are things I got from my father.'

'Your mother was white: Where did she come from?'

'I don't know. By the time I knew her she was speaking Paiute and wore native dress.'

'So where did the name 'Joe Savidge' come from? Was Savidge your mother's maiden name?'

'No. Don't know what her name was. She didn't talk about her earlier life. Seems she'd been on a wagon train that had run into trouble. What kind I don't know. Anyways, she was given refuge by the Paiute and one of the braves took

140

her as wife. In those days there was little contact with whites so little hope of her returning to her own kind. When I came along, I was raised in the Indian style on the reservation at Walker Lake. As a youngster it was normal for me to learn the secrets of the desert, to know where there are seeps and hidden tanks in the rocks. None of them holds much but there's enough to keep a critter from dying of thirst, man or beast.'

He chuckled. 'That's why you don't see whites out here. Only animals and Indians know where the seeps are. Even when I've lost my bearings and don't know where water is, I can read animal sign like I been doing on the journey out here. Sometimes, without the help of sign, I can smell it. On the trek out our mules were doing the same thing.'

She nodded. 'Amazing.'

'There are many things in nature that the redman is attuned to that the white man has no idea of. My people knew of these things and were renowned in their knowledge of the terrain. Your famous

Kit Carson used Utes as trackers whenever he could.'

'You still haven't explained where the name 'Joe Savidge' came from.'

'The Indian agent at the reservation had commented to some passing soldiers about my appearance, looking white and all. By then Mother had passed away and I was a fully-fledged brave. But the soldiers carted me away and fixed me up in a missionary school. I learned English and was set on the path of becoming a white man.'

He chuckled. 'Huh, the kids referred to me as the Savage, sometime times even The Filthy Savage — you know how mean kids can be — and my first schoolteacher either misheard or had a sense of humour because she entered my name on the register as Savidge.'

'I see. And your first name?'

'The teacher was a Mormon and gave me Joseph as my first name. You know, after Joseph Smith, the founder of Mormonism.'

'And you didn't want to run away,'

she prompted, 'back to your tribe?'

'When you're a kid you can accept what happens to you, as though it's just part and parcel of this thing called Life. I've heard of native children being bullied into abandoning their traditional ways. That didn't happen to me. I was simply intent on surviving. Took things as they came. And, at least at missionary school, I had a full belly instead of the scrapings you can get dished out on the reservation. When my school days were over I joined the army. Learnt how to handle horses and guns. By then I could pass as hundred per cent white so my fellow soldiers didn't know of my origins and I didn't see cause to enlighten them. My past was becoming a distant memory anyway. Things were OK for some time. Even got promotion.'

'If you were doing so well, why are you not still dressed in army blue?'

'Said 'so long' to my army uniform when I found myself getting increasingly involved in campaigns against the

Indians. Upshot, I mustered myself out at the first opportunity.'

'You were required to fight the Paiutes?'

'No, Apaches and Comanche. But they are of the People too.'

'The People? What does that mean?'

'For a long time our tribes fought each other but in more recent times there has developed the notion that we are all one; that we should not wage war with each other. And together we, that is all natives in North America, bear the name the People. So it was wrong for me to take arms against them, simply because of the colour of their skin. And simply because the white man wants their land.'

'And since then?' she asked. 'How have you got by?'

'Ain't much you can do in the white man's Nevada outside of mining. So that's been my trade, I suppose you'd call it. I've wielded a pick extracting silver, nickel, copper, quartz. You name it, I've hacked it out of the earth. Bad conditions, hard work but you can earn enough to fill your belly. That's what I was doing out at Bullionville when I ran into a spot of trouble that earned me forced passage to Pioche. And that's when you found me, stumbling into your establishment. You know the rest.'

'I wished you'd have told us this earlier.' It was Valeur, now stirring under the blanket. 'About being an Indian and all. Not that I've doubted you but I'd have felt a lot more confident.'

'You never asked,' Savidge said. He thought on the matter. 'But having these words with you here I'm beginning to realize I have hidden my background. That is, consciously hidden it. And that is fast becoming a source of shame. I prided myself I wasn't hiding it, just didn't make it obvious. But I can now see I was fooling myself and I was definitely obscuring it. Except to folks like Flying Dog.' He chuckled. 'Huh, the old guy could tell immediately. Gave us a bond.'

'Was he Paiute?' she asked.

'No, Shoshoni. But a brother none the less.' The memory of his burying the old man rose in his mind. 'Said Indian words over him after I'd put him under.'

'The way you talked of him,' Holiday said, 'right from the beginning I sensed there was something strong between you. Something more than just between a lodger and somebody supplying accommodation.'

'Yes. I'm acknowledging what I am and I'm going to stand up for it.'

At that point Valeur began to move and Savidge watched him haul himself into a sitting position. 'And how are you now, Anton?'

'Recovering. As I said, these bouts work themselves out.' He spent a moment with his thoughts, then added, 'One thing this exercise has taught me, *m'sieur*. the desert can be a prison in a way I could not have imagined. The nature of the desert is a ruthless turnkey that can lock a man within its

146

confines, tease him with the open distances, then torture its prisoner to death with thirst. It is a godsend that I met you to aid me in this endeavour. For that alone, I thank you, *M'sieur le Brave*.'

13

The Frenchman recovered enough to take food. Wrapped in a blanket he was still shivering despite the latent heat of the desert.

'Holiday tells me we're almost there,' he said weakly.

'Don't bother yourself with that anymore,' Savidge said. 'We're turning back. There's still a good section of a day's travel required to get to the Wells — and the sun gets worse the nearer to the centre of the desert. Acts like a mirror and catches every ray of sun that's going and focuses it. A hellhole like that ain't for you in your condition. Best we draw a line under the expedition and get you back to a doc as soon as possible.'

Despite his weakness Valeur got agitated. 'No! We can't give up now! We've got to carry on!'

'Listen, I know that going back now means that I'll be losing half my fee,' Savidge said, 'but if we carry on and you die out here, I'll be losing that anyhow. No, it's best we get you back to where you can be looked after properly.'

Valeur didn't seem to hear him. Instead, he peered into the darkness of their backtrail then looked at Holiday. 'These fellows who came out with you, were they French?'

'No. Just looked like ordinary guys, I've told you.'

The Frenchman looked at his guide. 'We've still got to press on. I'll be all right, Joe. Just have to take it easy.'

'It ain't workable. You can't take it easy out here. It's not my intention to be rude but, fact is, Anton, you're a liability now.'

'I'll double your fee,' Valeur blurted.

Savidge looked at the Frenchman quizzically. 'You'll double my fee just so that you can write — a history book? I don't believe it!' He cast a glance at

Holiday. 'These fellers out there, they look like bookwriters too?'

She smiled. 'More like saddle bums.'

Savidge looked back at Valeur. 'And why, just now, did you ask if they were French?'

The man shrugged.

'Don't treat me like I just come down the pike, Anton. You're hiding something, *mon ami*. I figure it's about time you came clean. Those guys back there are after something. This place is dangerous. A place where lots of people never get out alive. That's why nobody travels into it. It's the easiest thing to die out here and those guys back there would not be exposing themselves to dangerous conditions like this for peanuts. Plus, it's something for which they were prepared to kidnap our lady here. And something for which you're now prepared to double my fee.'

'And it's got something to do with the coins,' Holiday added.

'Yeah,' Savidge went on. 'They want

what you're after. So exactly what are you after, *m'sieur*? Gotta be something big, something that you're prepared to pay me a grand to help you get. Now's the time to tell us. Why the hell are we out here?'

Valeur ferreted through his pockets and took out the coins, studying them before passing one over to Savidge. 'The effigy on the face — it's that of Napoleon. You have heard about him?'

'I might be an Indian but I ain't totally uneducated.'

'And the Napoleonic Wars, you know much about them?'

'Remember something from school.'

'In that case you'll know that that conflict, which had been going on for two decades or so in Europe, was finally ended at the Battle of Waterloo.'

'Yeah, I know that much.'

'Well, it is widely known that when Blücher and Wellington beat Napoleon's ass at Waterloo, the self-styled emperor was exiled for a second and last time. But one of the incidental

151

details they may not have told you at school was that his officers were also exiled. Courtesy of his captors, Napoleon was sent to the island of St Helena but his unfortunate officers had nowhere to go. None of the European countries wanted anything to do with them.'

'Understandable,' Savidge said. 'Their armies had invaded and wrought mayhem in most countries across the Continent.'

'So,' Valeur continued, 'with nobody willing to take them — your country — the US offered them sanctuary, and for that purpose allocated land in Alabama as accommodation for them. As a result the grateful officers and their families came over and set up home in Mobile, Demopolis and a couple of other settlements.

'Snag was, it transpired there were legal problems over the deeds of the land allocation. Mistakes had been made by the US bureaucracy and my countrymen were forced to leave. Stuck in a strange country, they dispersed. Some integrated in existing local American communities. Some headed for Canada where there were already French communities. Odd families would drop off and settle where they could along the way. The rest set off on other long hauls, to all points of the compass.

'Now, Napoleon's army had been a raggle-taggle bunch as might be expected. After all, it was his second army, having been hastily gathered after his escape from his first spell of exile on the island of Elba. However, many of his officers were well off and they brought their money with them when they came to the States. But, as the US was funding them, it had been in their interests to plead poverty so they kept quiet about their major assets.

'There were several caches hidden away. Now there was a rumour that one of the largest hoards — in the shape of golden napoleon coins — was aboard a wagon train heading west. The fascinating thing is the wagon train disappeared from the face of the earth along with all the trekkers and the store of wealth. I have been studying this matter for years. There is no evidence they settled anyplace. So what happened to them and the money? My researches led me to two possibilities. They were subjected to attack by Indians, the folks killed, their belongings looted. Then time and weather removed any vestiges of their ever being there. But I don't think that's what happened. I have been touring the West for so long I'm sure I would have heard a clue, a whisper, somewhere in all the Indian tales I've been listening to.'

'So?' Savidge pressed.

'I reckon they were merely hit by arduous conditions, some natural calamity like a sandstorm. Or they simply lost their bearings in a desert. Or some highly contagious, quickly spreading illness struck: cholera, something like that. Whatever happened to them they were in some barren region, fifty or a hundred miles, even more, from any regular trails. With no observers of their misfortunes, their fate would go unrecorded. And being a long distance from civilization would explain how come no sign has ever been seen of them. As they fell there would be carrion creatures waiting to eat any remains. Then wind and moving sands constantly shifting the terrain would cover up whatever was left of them, their wagons and livestock.'

Savidge nodded. 'Possible. Sand drifts are constantly changing the landscape. I've known of sand that's completely immersed wagons in no time at all.'

'*Oui, m'sieur*. Depends on the looseness of sand, strength and convergence of winds and so on.'

'And that's what this is all about? The possibility — the crazy, remote possibility — of finding some Napoleonic treasure trove?'

'I wouldn't express it exactly in those words.'

'Listen,' Savidge said, 'in the face of conditions that can completely obliterate any clues — conditions that we've both described — any search for them is even more of a wild goose chase.' He shook his head in increasing disbelief 'Haven't you ever heard of a needle in a haystack? I tell you, pal, I'm sure glad I'm working for a fixed salary on this and that my earnings aren't dependent on finding some mythical Eldorado. Yeah, that's what you've been looking for — a needle in a haystack.'

'I might have agreed with you, *m'sieur*. Up till I got the cable from Holiday and I spoke with the old man back in Pioche. The coins and his story have been the first tangible sign.'

'The coins look real enough, but the odds are the old codger could have been spinning you a tale.'

'I don't think so.'

'Did you pay him anything?'

'Bought him a bottle of liquor.'

Savidge grunted. 'The odds have just gone up on his spinning you a yarn. Figure he'd tell you anything you wanted to hear if there was something in it for him. Guys like him are born time-servers.'

'So what are you saying?' the Frenchman

asked, a quizzical expression marking his features.

'There's still a deal to go to get to the Wells,' Savidge said. 'That's what I'm saying. And it's gonna get worse. Plus we only got supplies for two to meet the needs of three.'

'I'm sorry,' Holiday said. 'It's all my fault.'

'No, it's not,' Savidge said. 'Don't blame yourself. You couldn't help it. I'm just stating the facts of the situation. And looming large in the calculation is Anton's poor health.'

'So?' Valeur pressed.

'This really is a fool's errand, Anton. You gotta face it.'

Panic flared across Valeur's face. 'If we find this hoard,' he spluttered, 'I'll . . . I'll give you half!'

'A half of nothing!' Savidge whispered derisively. 'Huh, don't seem much of a bargain to me.'

Valeur dropped his head into his hands and Savidge looked at him for a long time.

Holiday broke the silence with, 'If

157

we're nearly there, I can't see why we can't press on.'

Savidge turned his attention to her as he thought over the situation. Then let out a sigh and looked back at Valeur. 'OK. You're obviously keen to see this thing through whatever the cost. And I have to admit you were trusting enough to give me half the fee before we set out. Suppose the least I can do is pursue the damn thing to the end. If only to prove to you what a farce the whole enterprise is. But I can't guarantee anything, not with you in your condition. If you don't make it, you've only yourself and your obsession to blame.'

★ ★ ★

They were travelling raggedly in single file when, ahead of the other two, Savidge stopped and pointed into the distance.

'What is the matter, *m'sieur?*' Valeur asked. Then, peering in the indicated direction, he could make out a mysterious rounded mass. '*Mon Dieu*! What is that?'

It seemed alive and the longer he looked at it the more organic it seemed to be. It was growing — and coming nearer.

'Dust storm,' Savidge said. He studied it. 'Fingers crossed, there's a chance it might miss us.'

But, as the wind picked up around them and he felt the sting of bullet-fast pieces of sand, he knew they were at least in the periphery of the turbulence. And it could get worse.

He looked around. Noting there was no cover, he spotted a gap between two mounds of sand and pointed to it. 'In between those dunes!' he shouted above the increasing noise. 'Not much, but better than nothing.'

The animals were becoming difficult to handle as they were led to the indentation. He quickly extracted the headpieces that he had prepared back in Pioche and threw them at his

159

companions. 'Over the mules' heads,' he shouted.

With the speed of someone who knew what he was doing he took out ropes and hobbled the animals' legs.

'Now lie down,' he shouted above the increasing roar. He took out two bags and handed them to Holiday and Valeur in turn.

'Over your heads and make them as airtight as possible!' he shouted before pulling up his bandanna. Then he dropped to the ground and, pulling his hat tight around his face, rolled into a foetal ball.

The noise was deafening and, with their faces masked, it was stifling.

They may have lain that way for a quarter of an hour. Time had become meaningless. Savidge only raised his hat and carefully lowered his bandanna when he reckoned it was very safe to do so. The storm had subsided but there were still fine particles hanging in the air — enough to cut visibility by diffusing the sunlight; enough to irritate the back of his throat.

He scrabbled across to the other two. 'All clear,' he croaked.

For a few minutes the trio coughed uncontrollably. Finally Savidge grimaced, got to his feet, and wiped sandy spittle from his lips. 'You two OK?'

When it was clear they were over the ordeal he crossed to the mules. One by one he removed their protective covers, then wiped their eyes and mouths with a wet cloth. 'Our transport's survived too,' he concluded.

He looked around the scene. Very little remained of the two original sand dunes while the rest of the landscape had been completely reconfigured. 'We've been lucky, folks. I've known of folks buried alive under a mother like that one. And other poor souls who've been sucked upwards and thrown hundreds of yards to their deaths. By any measure, we came out of it OK.'

They sipped at canteens to clear their throats.

When Savidge had given the mules

some licks of water from a cupped hand, he looked back. 'It's been an ordeal but there's been no damage and there's a bonus. If those bozos who kidnapped Holiday were following us, they'll never find our tracks now.'

14

It was early morning and canteens were bouncing empty from pommels. Savidge's skills at finding water seemed to have abandoned him.

'How much further?' the Frenchman wanted to know.

'I've said I reckon noon should make it,' Savidge said, squinting into the distance. 'But take heart, my friend. By my figuring there's one more water source on the way. I'm looking for it now.'

His planting of the seed of hope seemed to give his companions new heart. Then, half an hour on, he glimpsed a change in colour ahead. As they neared it had the appearance of vegetation. Vegetation!

'Look, green,' he croaked, pointing forward. 'That means water.'

But when he reached the discolouration, he could see it merely marked the dip of a dried-up waterhole. The pale weed surrounding it was dead. He stumbled across the cracks and dropped to the ground. He started clawing at the crumbly ground in search of moisture deep down.

He didn't know how long he was scraping, watched by expectant eyes; but he did know there was no sign of the life fluid. The texture several feet down was as dry as the surface. And all he had to show for it was sore fingers.

He looked up at the once expectant faces, now showing nothing but dismay.

'Water or no water we're still gonna have to rest a spell,' he said. 'Then we press on, at our best pace. Don't worry. We're gonna make it.'

Valeur was swaying, all his gentlemanly graces gone. 'I think you might have been right after all about turning back. I'm sorry for arguing with you. I don't think I'm gonna make it.'

'If you can hold out till we get to the Wells,' Savidge said, 'there's all the shade you could want, and there's as much cool water as you could crave.'

'Shade, water,' Valeur mouthed weakly. 'Wouldn't have thought that heaven could exist in a place like this but the picture you paint, it sounds like it.'

★ ★ ★

Their pace was slowing and they'd covered no more than a couple of miles since their last stop of several hours before.

Savidge had taken off his hat and was sleeving sweat from his face, when Valeur shouted.

'Look, *mes amis*!'

Savidge squinted in the direction in which the Frenchman was pointing. He could make out some blurred spots to their rear.

'It'll be those guys who kidnapped Holiday!' Valeur said, concern edging his voice.

'Don't think so,' Savidge said. 'That sandstorm will have hit them as bad as us. After a mother like that they're gonna be pretty lost. This is a big, featureless place. So don't worry yet. I don't think it's them.'

'Are you sure?'

'No. But if it's them and they're aiming to follow us, they've been mighty lucky.'

'Providence can make for a man what he himself cannot do, *m'sieur*,' Valeur said.

'Maybe, but let's wait and see,' Savidge said, reaching for the butt of the carbine holstered on his mule. 'Meantime, prepare your weapon.'

As he studied the advancing figures, Savidge rubbed his chin, conscious of the rasp of thick whiskers.

'Something about their movement,' he said after some contemplation.

They remained silent in the heat. Holiday fanned herself. Valeur wiped his face.

Then Savidge exclaimed, 'They're Indians!'

'What do we do?' the Frenchman said. 'Keep our guns at the ready?'

'No point,' Savidge said, counting their number. 'There's too many of 'em. What's more, showing we're ready to use our weapons might antagonize them.' He lowered his own gun. 'We just sit tight and see what happens. Like you might say, let's see what Providence has in store for us.'

It took a long time for the group to get near. Savidge watched them draw to a halt when they were some twenty yards away, and he laughed. He stood, raised a flat palm and said something in dialect.

The band resumed their approach, one breaking away from the others and presenting himself before Savidge. The two men gripped forearms in obvious friendship.

Savidge told his companions to rest up while he and the Indian walked a little distance away together. The two men dropped to the ground and sat cross-legged before each other.

They spoke for maybe a quarter of an hour. Then they rose and returned.

Savidge took some handfuls of jerky from a bag and passed it to the man who distributed it amongst his comrades.

Then the Indians offered water and Savidge took a long, quenching drink.

Despite their need, his companions looked apprehensive at the sight of the grubby, animal skin bags.

Savidge noted the grimaces on their faces. 'If you don't drink you're gonna cause offence.' Then, he added in a whisper, 'Even if you can't face it, take a short drink. It's polite. Besides, given the situation we're in, it could save your lives.'

While they hesitantly sampled the liquid, Savidge exchanged words in dialect with the Indian leader. The latter then gave instructions to an underling who set about topping up the trio's canteens.

That done, the two leaders clenched forearms once more. And the Indians loped away. Savidge watched them until they were mere formless shapes in the distance, then turned to his fellow travellers.

'That was Red Coyote,' he explained. 'An old friend from the Walker Lake reservation.' He shook his head. 'Real amazing to come across him out here.'

'Of your tribe?' Holiday asked.

'No, they're Bannocks. But close kin.'

'And what brings him into this God-forsaken place?' Valeur asked.

'This 'God-forsaken place', as you call it, is their heritage,' Savidge said. 'They've chosen to live the traditional way on land that once belonged to them.'

'Belonged to them?' Valeur queried.

'By natural right,' Savidge snapped, 'and this is about the only place the redman can roam unmolested. And that's only because the white man doesn't want the land yet!'

'Can they just leave a reservation like that?' Holiday asked. 'I thought they were under some kind of government orders. Signed treaties, something like that.'

'True, and their white masters don't

like them cutting loose. But as long as the runaways are small in number and don't cause any trouble, the officials turn a blind eye. And Red Coyote and his braves are not the kind to cause trouble.'

'They can't be getting enough to survive if you had to give them some of our precious jerky,' Valeur observed.

'They didn't need it. It was just a courtesy token, like the water.' He eyed the other two. 'But in our case, the water was more than a token — despite your obvious distaste. Think on it. There's a strong chance we could be dying of thirst now without it.'

'Did you ask them if they've seen any other whites out here?' Valeur wanted to know.

'I did and they haven't,' Savidge said, taking the reins of his mule and resuming his plodding.

15

With nowhere to get shade they had no recourse but to trudge on through the inferno of the noon sun. Fatigue slowed them to the extent that it was well into the afternoon that Savidge saw what looked like irregular shapes on the horizon. Heads down, the others hadn't seen anything and, rather than raise hopes, he said nothing. Such contours waving in the heat-haze could mean anything. His experience in deserts had made him well aware of the mind's capacity to play tricks. But eventually the things sharpened up. At first one building, then quickly others.

It was then he stopped and drew the attention of his companions to it.

★　★　★

An hour on they were staggering towards the complex of white adobe buildings. The detritus that accompanies one-time occupancy was evident in empty cans, the remains of broken tools, bits of wagons, and shattered furniture.

'This is it, M'sieur Valeur,' Savidge said, raising his arms in triumph. 'The legendary Vegas Wells.'

The Frenchman looked around for a few seconds, then dropped to his knees in exhaustion.

'Let's get Anton into shade,' Savidge said.

That done he set off. 'Now we look for water. This is when we cross our fingers, gal.'

With Holiday trailing behind he made his way through the ghost town and into a walled area where he knew the wells were located. 'Technically they're known as artesian springs,' he said. 'They were surrounded by a wall to keep out animals.'

'Animals? Out here?'

'You'd be surprised, ma'am. Burros, for instance.'

'Burros?'

'Yeah. They run wild out here. Figure the Spanish brought 'em over in the old days. Having to survive by themselves, somehow the critters have adapted to the harsh environment with the result they got the constitution of camels. It's said they can last the best part of a week without water.'

He looked down each well in turn. Each consisted of a deep narrow hole with support and wooden beam across the top. And each drew a blank until he said, 'Here, I don't have to see it, I can smell it,' as he leaned over one of the wells. 'Let's find some container.'

A brief rummage through some of the buildings turned up a dusty pail. He took some stout rope from one of their mules, fixed one end to the pail. He checked the sturdiness of one of the beams. 'This one will do.'

He fixed the rope to the beam and clambered down into the darkness. It was difficult as parts of the walls had crumbled and there was debris at the bottom, but there was enough leeway for him to claim some water.

'Hoist away,' he shouted when the pail was as full as he could get it.

Back at the top he sampled some. 'Drinkable. Come on, let's get some to our French friend. I figure he's in most need.'

'Not wise to drink too much,' he said, when the three of them were together again. 'A little and often, as they say.'

Minutes later the trio were sitting in the shade of a building, their backs against the wall. They'd all taken a few voracious gulps and doused their faces, necks and arms. Eyes closed, they revelled in its touch.

Savidge tethered the mules in shade, unpacked and watered them.

Back at the well he took another drink and luxuriated in the water that he poured over his bared head.

'Any ideas where to start looking for your cache, *m'sieur*?' Holiday asked, her eyes still closed as she savoured the

174

liquid oozing down her throat.

'Figure that's low in our priorities at the moment,' Savidge put in. 'We have to see to the animals — feed 'em and make sure they're comfortable. After all, they got us here. They deserve some fussing. Then we'll keep in the shade, eat and rest. When we've all had a good sleep we'll be able better to apply our minds to the search. Time is no longer pressing. If the cache is here, for sure it ain't gonna run away.'

★ ★ ★

The next day, thoroughly rested, they scouted out the place roughly before conducting a systematic search. Here and there bleached bones, animal and some that looked human. All buildings were still standing, although roofless, with glass long-gone from windows and paint coming away from wood in flakes and curls.

They explored the interiors. Beads, pots, broken bottles, remnants of furniture, pieces of threadbare cloth. Savidge found a curved section of metal and, close by, a much dented round object.

'What are these oddities?' he asked.

Valeur inspected the bowed piece of metal. 'Well, this looks a like a breastplate. See the holes for fixing it to the chest?' He looked closely at the rounded object. 'And this looks like it could once have been a conquistador's helmet. Guess they were left by the original Spanish explorers.'

'So at least there's evidence of the Spanish being here,' Savidge said, 'if not the French.'

They toured the building shells. Pervasive sand drifts stacked high against the remaining walls, indicating that, whatever place of habitation it had been for all the varied travellers or settlers who had come to it, the desert was gradually reclaiming its own.

The site lay in a shallow valley, the surrounding bare landscapes showing hardly a trace of green.

Completing their search for the time being and getting nowhere, they congregated together for a bite to eat.

'Nobody's told me what this place is exactly,' Holiday said. 'And why would anyone build such a place in the middle of nowhere?'

'Spanish explorers discovered it way back in the old days,' Valeur said. 'It was they named it Vegas Wells.'

Savidge raised a hand, a puzzled look coming to his face. 'Hang on there, pal. I thought the first you knew of this was when you turned up in Pioche. Holiday had told you about the coins and that ailing prospector told you where he'd found them.'

Valeur fidgeted. 'I've done some reading on it.'

'When did you get chance to do some reading on it? You'd be hard pushed to find a book in Pioche, never mind some history book describing Vegas Wells.'

Valeur paused, then said, 'Fact is, I've been researching the region for a long time.'

'You never told us that.'

'I knew *of* the place,' Valeur said. 'But little more. I knew that since the Spanish had discovered it, it has been marked with some imprecision on maps. But it was all very vague and its *exact* location has not been known.'

'What do you mean nobody knew its exact location?' Savidge put in. 'I brought you right to it.'

Valeur coughed. 'Yes, well . . . '

Savidge looked knowledgeably at the woman, and winked. 'He means whites didn't know where it was.'

'Then from time to time,' Valeur went on, 'travellers lost in the desert would return to civilization with tales about coming across a lost oasis. Some returned and tried to settle here. But, despite the ample water conditions proved too hostile.'

'Not forgetting Indian attacks,' Savidge interrupted. 'Don't forget them. See, my dear Holiday, the redskins didn't cotton to whites encroaching on their land.' He pulled a wry face and added,

178

'For the life of me I can't think why.'

He finished a strip of jerky and washed it down with water. 'This has been a real pie-in-the-sky caper, Anton. Yet you've put a great deal of research into the area and certainly about Vegas Wells. Seems to me you've got more than these coins to go on. Is there no other evidence? No other clues?'

Valeur remained quiet.

'You sure play your cards close to your chest, don't you, pal?' Savidge observed. 'You didn't tell us you were chasing some hidden cache until I virtually forced it out of you. And I think you're still hiding something from us.'

'There is one snippet I may have overlooked to tell you,' Valeur admitted.

'And that is?'

'These French families who left the original communities in Alabama looking for somewhere else to settle. There was a particular group that aroused my interest. A small assemblage. Can't be sure but could have been as little as two wagons. Set out heading west for San Francisco.'

'And what did you think was so interesting about them?'

'This particular company of voyagers consisted of General d'Escalier and his family. From correspondence they sent while passing through towns with mail offices, I've been able to trace part of their journey. But I can find no record of them ever reaching their destination. Or, in fact, any destination.'

'Hell, they could have fetched up anywhere between Laramie and the coast!' Savidge observed.

'True, but d'Escalier was a big name, he being one of Napoleon's right-hand officers. It is unlikely that if he settled, the family name would not have surfaced sometime, somewhere. But it hasn't. No, the way I see it something unrecorded happened to that small wagon train. And, from my studies I concluded that there's every chance they had tried to cross this desert. That means that Vegas Wells was highly likely to have been on their route.'

'And you think this is as far as they got?'

'A strong possibility. The two recovered coins indicate a big chance they were here. And we've seen human bones. Some of them could be the remains of the French travellers. If they were in a bad way, it would have been logical for them to stay; to try to survive here as many had done before them. At least here they would have been sure of water. With an uncertain future and virtually imprisoned, they would have stashed the money for safe-keeping.'

'Those bits of human skeletons we've seen,' Savidge said, 'could belong to any poor souls who stumbled across the place. Not necessarily your French folk.'

Valeur nodded. 'And fifty years on with carrion feeding off them and this harsh sun, there'd be nothing to identify them as French trekkers, I agree. But we are here, so let us be thorough in establishing whether our own journey has been wasted or not.'

In the afternoon the three made another circuit of the complex.

'I reckon this is where the old-timer found the coins,' Valeur said when they were near the remains of what had once been a thriving orchard.

'If I was burying a cache that I was hoping to come back to,' Savidge said, 'I don't think I'd pick a decaying orchard. Not many notable features for me to be able to remember an exact location. Then, the trees could well have been blossoming and one doesn't know how it might have changed when one came back to it. I'd go for something less changeable.'

'I agree,' Valeur said. He pointed to an area of sloping ground to the north a little distance from the main complex: a cemetery with a score or so of stones and wooden markers. 'That looks more promising. A grave doesn't change much over time. Easy to remember and locate. A name for example.'

'Do you have a name?'

'No.'

'Are you sure?'

'I have nothing left to hide, *m'sieur*. All that I know, you now know.' Tired, he hunkered down while Savidge and Holiday strolled over and looked at the simple memorials.

'Any French names amongst them?' Valeur asked. 'That would at least tell us something.'

'Can't read them,' Savidge said after some investigation. 'They're all illegible.'

Sand had blasted away the lettering on stone markers and the wooden ones were crumbling; all angled and forlorn.

'The only thing they tell us,' Holiday added, 'is that some poor critters were here long enough for the cycle of life and death to turn. And for them, the big adventure was over, their only remaining task to keep a permanent vigil beneath the sand.'

'Amen,' Savidge said histrionically, his eyebrows having risen at the sound of something poetic.

Valeur stood up and looked across the vista of baked land beyond, then his gaze returned to the grave markers. 'More to the point, a grave is a good way of hiding something you don't want people other than yourself to find.'

'Maybe,' Savidge said, 'but if we've got to go through all these graves, we're gonna have our work cut out.'

The Frenchman scanned the vicinity. 'Let's find something to dig with and make a start while there's still light.'

'I spotted the crumbling remains of a wagon when we first arrived,' Savidge said. 'Its wheel staves should provide workable digging tools.'

16

Come noon the three had poked and dug well into around half the graves.

Savidge paused in his labour and hunkered down to take a breather. 'Just had an idea,' he suddenly said. 'You carry on here while I try something out.'

Valeur relaxed and, wiping his brow, leant on the robust hunk of wood he had been using to dig with. 'What's on your mind?'

Savidge pointed to the big well. 'I been thinking. You know, if I was intent on hiding something I'd certainly investigate to see if the well served my purpose. A well would stand the test of time and be easy to recognize when I came back.'

'Maybe,' the Frenchman said with a nod, and resumed his digging while Savidge walked down the avenue towards the well.

'I need a break,' Holiday said, laying down her stick and following him.

At the well Savidge straddled the adobe coping and gripped the rope he had fixed for the raising of the bucket. After checking its capability to hold his weight he began to work his way down the hole.

He let himself down, getting a little leverage with his feet against the rough walls. Every few feet he braced his feet and checked the sides. At first it was easy to visually check the surfaces for signs of disturbance. But the lower he got the darker it became.

'You OK?' Holiday shouted when he had disappeared into the gloom.

'Yeah, but no sign yet.'

Their voices echoed up and down the shaft.

He continued downwards. If he were hiding a fortune down here, where would he conceal it for the best? He felt along the walls for some irregularity. He could recognize where bits had crumbled away naturally but could find nothing that indicated some intentional re-working of the wall faces in order to hide something.

Eventually his feet entered water and he touched bottom. He explored as much as he could in the darkness, then looked up at the small circle of light. 'I'm coming back up.'

At the top he hauled himself over the coping and dropped onto the sand with his back against the wall.

After a rest he made his way to the cemetery where Valeur was still poking the ground with a stave. Every now and again the Frenchman would get his stick deep enough to unearth a sizeable chunk of hard soil.

He spotted Savidge. 'No luck, *m'sieur*?'

'No,' Savidge said, as he scouted about to find his discarded piece of wood. Then he joined the other in digging.

A half-hour on he stopped and sleeved sweat from his brow.

'I'm still not satisfied,' he said.

He dropped his makeshift digging tool and headed back to the well.

'What's on your mind?' Holiday asked, attaching herself once again to his side.

'Something I overlooked,' he said.

Back at the well he gripped the rope and worked his way once more into the hole. At the bottom he stood on rubble with the water lapping round his boots while he waited for his eyes to adjust to the darkness. Then he bent down and began feeling the base on which he stood. His fingers told him he was standing on a flat rock which was somewhat smaller than the circumference of the hole so that there was a noticeable gap around it. He dropped to his knees, plunged his hands into the water to explore the hidden underside.

Felt like there was something underneath!

He stepped off the flat rock, stood against the wall and gripped the slab. Despite the heat of the desert way above his head, the water was cold and his fingers were beginning to numb.

The wedge was heavy but he was able

to lever it partially at an angle. Then, with legs wide apart, he managed eventually to raise it enough so he could lean it against the wall. Once again his fingers explored the unseen space under the water; and he sensed a solid regular shape.

Metal? A box?

He couldn't see it, but whatever it was he could move it slightly.

He hauled himself back up the well and took a length of rope from the supplies now stacked in one of the buildings.

'Tell Anton I've found something,' he said to Holiday. 'It's heavy so it'll need at least two pairs of hands. But don't know what it is, so tell him not to get too excited for no reason.'

Back down the well he worked the rope round four sides of the box, tied it to the central rope, then worked his way back to the top. The Frenchman joined him and the two hauled on the rope.

They could hear water splashing at the bottom as it dripped from the rising container, and debris thudding to the bottom as the thing bumped and scraped the wall on its ascent.

When it reached the top, Savidge leant over the wall to heave it clear.

'This has to be it,' Valeur breathed, the quiver of excitement in his voice.

It was easy for Savidge to wrench apart the crumbling clasp; and he flipped open the lid to reveal it to be full of coins.

Valeur dropped to his knees. '*Mon Dieu!*'

'Well, I'll be a son of a gun,' Savidge muttered. 'You weren't crazy after all.'

The Frenchman dipped his hands into the box and began repeatedly cascading the wet coins from hand to hand. The others joined him in getting the feel of the fortune.

Savidge held a fistful and stared at Valeur. 'Now we've found what we've been after,' he said, 'you willing to stand by your offer of shares?'

'Of course, *m'sieur*. Half each.'

Savidge nodded. 'That makes me a partner, don't it?'

'*Certainement.*'

'With full voting rights?'

'Of course.'

Savidge looked at Holiday, winked, then returned his gaze to the Frenchman. 'In that case I vote we take a third each. Holiday here deserves a full cut. If she hadn't gone out of her way to inform you about what had come into her possession we wouldn't be here now.'

The notion was enough to take the Frenchman aback.

'Namely a third of the surplus,' Savidge went on. 'That surplus after you've subtracted your costs.'

Valeur thought on it and said, 'Of course, you're right, *m'sieur*. Yes, you are correct. Such a dividing of the booty, it is fair.'

He began examining several coins in turn, inspecting the image of the emperor, reading the wording round the edges.

Savidge lay on his back and stared at the cloudless sky. Somehow the heat and the sun didn't bother him any more. 'How much do you think we'll get for them?'

'When an assayer has checked they are pure gold — which they are, I can tell by the dates — we'll get the market rate. But I hope we find a buyer wealthy enough to purchase some of them for what they are, historical artefacts, and to keep them intact for posterity. Either way, we are set to get a fortune.'

'So they're worth more than the five dollars we rated them in our poker game!' Holiday commented. Then, with some bite in her voice, she added, 'You didn't quibble when I mentioned that figure.'

'No I didn't,' Valeur said. 'And for that little subterfuge I must apologize, my dear Holiday.'

'So,' she persisted, 'what kind of money are we talking about?'

'Their value is more like a hundred dollars each.'

Savidge whistled and it was quiet for a spell, the only sound the clink of coins as Valeur inspected them individually.

'And you're not a scholar from some high-falutin' French academy,' Savidge said after a while.

'Not from some French academy, that is true.'

'Huh!' Savidge snorted. 'Yet another — subterfuge!'

'I apologize for that little deception too. But it was not wholly a deception. I am a scholar in the sense that I started studying books, documents, maps and the rest. That makes me a student of sorts, doesn't it?'

'Started studying when?'

'When I got a whiff that there could be some hidden hoard out West.'

'Ha! Whiff? And where did you get that whiff?'

'Plying the Mississippi on a three-deck packet.'

Savidge laughed. 'You were a steamboat man! Not some French aristocrat after all!'

Valeur reflected on the words. 'A steamboat man? Not quite. Mind, we even made the New Orleans to Natchez run in less than eighteen hours once. That stood as the record for a time. But a steamboat man, in the sense that you meant it? Not as such, more a permanent passenger. Virtually resident on the gaming deck. Made more than a slender living.'

'So that's where you got your card-playing skills?' Holiday prompted.

Valeur nodded. 'There was always some businessman willing to part with his money at the card table.'

Savidge shook his head. 'Well, I'll be — ! Huh, a side-wheeler cardsharp!'

Valeur stiffened and looked up from the treasure trove. 'No, I am a gentleman, *m'sieur*! I may not be the aristocratic academic educated in Paris, an image I may have affected, but I am nevertheless a gentleman. There was no *sharpness* with the cards! The captain was happy to have me aboard as long as there was no cheating or scandal. Of course, he was also happy with the retainer I paid him.'

'And you're not even French?'

Savidge suggested.

'I am a proud Frenchman, *m'sieur*. Came to this country while still a young man.'

'So what set you on the trail of the coins?'

'Born in France and spent much time in Louisiana — New Orleans particularly — I was, *naturellemel*, steeped in French history, and knew the tales of French adventures in the New World. I'd *heard* of the exiled generals but had paid it no mind; that is until I found myself in conversation over drinks one night with a Louisianan businessman, himself a French settler. He was descended from one of Napoleon's officers and was a firm believer that a cache existed somewhere. In a drunken state he was merely rambling and expressed no desire to do anything about it. He was just delivering his favourite set tale, you know, the way any fellow does when he's in his cups. But his story made me wonder. I was bored with life aboard a Mississippi paddler and sensed adventure. My years of gaming had brought in a goodly amount, enough to finance my search and the fellow had imparted enough information to give me some starting points. Then it was a matter of combing records, documents, caches of letters. So I am a student in that sense, *mon ami*. I concerned myself with anywhere where the French had settled or passed through: New Orleans, Mobile, all over Louisiana.'

At that point the conversation was left hanging in the air.

Valeur completed his examination of the coins and stood up.

Savidge yawned.

Valeur stretched. 'So, when can we start back, Joe? Maybe tonight when it's — '

The words died in his throat.

There had been a crack, deafening in the quiet of the ghost town — a vicious sound that could only have emanated from a rifle — and Valeur whipped round to collapse in the sand.

17

Savidge dived to one side and rolled for cover behind the wall of the well.

'It's them,' Holiday said. 'The ones who kidnapped me.'

Neither Savidge or Valeur had been carrying weapons and their carbines were inaccessible, tucked away in the saddle boots that they had stored in one of the buildings.

'Stand up and show yourself,' a voice boomed. 'Or the woman gets the next one. And make it real slow. Anything else will earn you a slug too.'

Savidge hesitated before he complied. But he had no idea where the bushwhackers were or how near, so he concluded there was nothing for it but for him to rise, which he did slowly with his hands raised.

As he did so he saw two men advancing. Both had levelled guns.

One was a short, stocky fellow with a hard, pockmarked face. 'Nice to see you again, ma'am,' he said. Now leaning over the prone Frenchman, the woman said nothing, too concerned with removing his ornate vest and opening his shirt so that she could examine the wound in his side.

'We was unhappy you didn't want our company,' the other one said in mock offence. He was tall, with long greasy hair down to his shoulders. Despite his time in the desert his face was untarnished by the sun. 'Scooting the way you did, very ungracious of you. Thought we'd lost your tracks with that sandstorm but, never mind, we're all together again.'

He stared at Savidge with almost colourless eyes. 'And this is the guide we heard about, the one who knows the desert.'

Savidge made no comment while the short one advanced on Valeur and looked down at him. He kicked him to gain his attention. 'We been following you for quite a spell, Frenchie. You led us a merry dance. Traipsing from state to state, town to town. Hell, we've plumb wore out the map.'

'How did you know what was the object of my search?' Valeur asked weakly.

'You had to ask so many questions,' the tall one said. 'Specific questions — so specific that it didn't take too much thinking for us to work things out. Hell, it was no secret about what you were after. Just nobody believed the thing existed. But we figured there was a possibility. At least an intriguing prospect, shall we say? See, we asked our own questions. Guessed there might be something in it. But more important, we had time on our hands for such a business, didn't we, Mr Berens?'

'We had that,' the short one said. 'What Mr Trane means is that we had cause to make ourselves scarce, what with the law after us and all. Coming out this far west, especially losing ourselves in the desert, fitted very convenient into our needs.'

'Yeah,' the tall one said. 'Our mugs on posters all over the place to the East, from Louisiana to the Appalachians. Never been so popular. Where could we go to get away from the men with the tin stars? It was while we were pondering on that conundrum when we became intrigued by your investigations. So this caper, following you, fitted the bill, got us out of the way. Seeing as we had to make ourselves scarce, it was no skin off our nose to follow you. Could even be some cash profit in it for us as a bonus, we reckoned. As Mr Berens says, kinda convenient.'

He chuckled. 'Mind, it stretched our patience at times. Heck, there was spells when we too thought you were in cloud cuckoo land.' He edged over and looked at the box and its contents. 'But it's all been worthwhile, ain't it?' He laughed. 'At least worthwhile for *us*!'

'What we gonna do with them, Mr Trane?' the short one asked.

The leader stepped back. 'A bullet each should do the trick I think, Mr Berens,' he said in a low voice.

The squat man frowned. 'We don't have to kill 'em, boss. That'll put another murder charge around our necks.'

The leader laughed. 'What? Out here? Who's gonna know?'

'I got an idea. We can leave 'em here, boss, with no supplies or mules. That'll do it. We'll take all the canteens so they won't be able to take water with them. That way they'll never get back. Especially with the Frenchie wounded. They'll either die here and join the rest of the bones around the place, or out in the desert. Whichever way it falls, they'll be out of our hair and off our conscience.'

'Conscience?' the leader grunted. 'What kind of ten-dollar word is that? We got no truck with conscience, you bozo. You ought to know that by now.'

He shook his head and looked at Savidge. 'No. This guide of Valeur's ain't no parlour dandy.' He touched his forehead. 'He knows things about the desert. He's already proved that. If there's a way to get back without food or containers to hold water, he'll know it.'

'Do what you will with us,' Savidge interposed, 'but take the woman with you. At least save her.'

The piggy eyes of the short man roamed over Holiday's dishevelled form. 'I wouldn't mind saving her, boss — for myself!'

The tall one snorted. 'Hell, can't you get your brain out of your pants? Think we're crazy? She's a witness to whatever we do. She's got to be eliminated too.'

'Still, I can't kill a woman, boss.'

'OK, that'll be my job,' the tall one said in a tired, matter-of-fact tone. He pulled back the hammer and levelled his gun at Holiday. 'Only way is to make sure they never leave. I'll see to the woman. You put paid to the guide.'

Savidge looked at the threatening muzzle of the short man's gun. He had no weapon himself and there was too much distance between them for him to rush the man.

The leader's arm straightened in the direction of the cowering Holiday. 'Then it'll be my pleasure to finish off the Frenchie.'

Savidge did the only thing he could do in the circumstances and leapt forward to put his body in front of that of the woman in a last-ditch attempt.

But fate had other plans.

Two sounds disturbed the air at the same time. A second before the cocked gun fired there was sudden whoosh and an arrow entered the tall man's scrawny throat, its bloody point appearing on the other side. His gun was aiming harmlessly into the sky when it was triggered.

The short one whirled round and took an arrow in the eye. He died immediately, collapsing in a heap beside his companion who was writhing in the sand, gurgling his life away.

Savidge swung his head. 'Coyote!' he yelled when he spotted his friend, bow in hand, appearing from behind a nearby adobe wall.

Another redman with readied bow appeared, then the rest of the band revealed themselves, approaching behind their leader. Up close, Red Coyote looked down at the bloody havoc the two arrows had caused. He watched the tall one exhibit a final stiffening, his colourless, unseeing eyes still open.

The Indian waited for the telltale limpness before he spoke. 'We were approaching the Wells when we heard gunshot,' he said. 'Then we could see the difficulty our brother was in, so we made our advance quietly.'

'So quiet,' Savidge said. 'I wasn't aware of your coming.'

Red Coyote swept a bronzed arm over the bodies. 'These were the men who were trailing you?'

'Yeah. Thought we'd lost 'em after a sandstorm.'

The Indian walked up to the box and looked into it. 'And they were after these coins?'

'Yes,' Savidge said. 'They're rather ancient French coins. You're welcome to help yourself. I'm sure my friends will not argue if you take whatever you like in recompense.'

'We need no reward for helping a brother,' the Indian said. 'It is plain that the contents of the box are what you have been seeking and you have every right to it all.' He looked down at the now still bodies. 'But we will take the offenders' guns and other possessions, if our brother has no objection.'

Savidge shook his head. 'Be my guest.'

'Then we bury the bodies deep,' the Indian continued. 'We do not want to have to make explanation to reservation officials should they ever come this way.'

He said something in dialect and his men set about the task.

'How is your friend's wound?'

'Haven't had time to inspect it,' Savidge said.

Red Coyote dropped to his knees beside the woman who had opened

Valeur's shirt to reveal a bloody mess in his side. The Indian examined the wound. 'Not pleasant,' he said, 'but it has the appearance of a mere scoring across the flesh. One of our number is a shaman. He knows of these things and will be able to help.'

He indicated for one the Indians who took his leader's place beside the injured man. After a perusal he said something in dialect.

'Our brother here knows of a plant, the sap of which will aid the wound,' Red Coyote said by way of translation. 'He has seen one close by. If you can find something to use as a bandage, my man will collect the sap.'

'We're in your hands,' Savidge said.

'Meantime I will clean the wound,' Holiday said, reaching for a canteen.

18

Holiday and Valeur were sitting in the lobby of The Overlander. Savidge had mysteriously excused himself some time before. The trio's return through the desert had been slow and arduous but without mishap. Valeur's wound was now strapped up after being tended by a doctor.

Holiday nibbled a nail nervously as she eyed the front door. She was tense whenever Savidge left the building. He had spoken of unfinished business in Bullionville and she knew that whatever he planned involved danger.

'And how do you feel?' she asked Valeur, in an attempt to get her mind off its worrying track.

'Stiff, sore,' the Frenchman said, 'but otherwise OK. I don't know what that redman put on it but the doc said it was well on the way to healing. Said if he knew what the stuff was he could make some money bottling it.'

Suddenly Savidge appeared in the front doorway and relief was visible in the woman's face as he strode towards them, clasping an armful of canned peaches.

'What's this?' she asked.

'Kind of celebration,' he said, as he laid them on the table. 'I'll fetch a can-opener and spoons.'

She kissed his cheek while he was still bent over the table. 'You don't forget things, do you? You're an angel, Joe.'

'I'm glad you're recovering, Anton,' she said, as Savidge disappeared in the direction of the kitchen. 'Trouble is I'm being evicted, so you won't be able to remain here in The Overlander for long.' She paused, then added, 'But, thinking about it, it may be that Mr Wyler hasn't got any immediate plans for the place. In that case he'd probably let you keep your room for a spell.'

'Don't worry, my dear Holiday. I'm moving on.'

'Are you all right to travel?'

He touched his bandaged side and chuckled. 'I've travelled halfway across the desert with this, so riding out of town in a Concorde will be pure luxury.'

'What are you going to do now you are on the mend?' Savidge asked, as he returned with the implements.

'Liquidate some of my coins when I can find a reputable agent,' the Frenchman said.

By agreement they had split the cache into four, Valeur taking two tranches to cover his expenses.

'Just enough cash to finance further research,' he continued. 'But I aim to keep as many samples as I can. Then I'm going to write an academic paper for one of the historical journals.'

'I thought that was just a cover story while you were really chasing a fortune,' Savidge said, as he set about the task of opening the cans.

'It was. But the whole caper has got me interested now in finding out what I can about the d'Escalier wagon-train. I've become genuinely intrigued about the journey they made and their fate. If I can unearth the facts I might well return to France and deliver lectures as a proven academic.'

'You're joking,' Savidge observed.

'Not entirely,' Valeur said, as though affronted.

They delved into the syrupy fruits for a while. Then Valeur went on, 'My investigations might even necessitate another trek out to Vegas Wells. Will you be available as a guide, Joe?'

'I doubt it,' Savidge said.

'So what are you going to do, Joe?' Valeur asked.

'For a start I have to have the remainder of my cash. As I said before, I need a good horse and a pair of quality guns.'

'Yes, I remember,' the Frenchman said. 'I've still got some cash in the kitty. I'll make out a draft in your name to meet your requirements. You'll be able to cash it at the bank here in town.'

* ★ ★

That afternoon Savidge was at a desolate spot some distance from Pioche, just far enough to be out of earshot of the inhabitants, and was firing at cans he had collected from the town dump on his way out.

He was no stranger to wielding a gun; that is, on the shooting range. In such circumstances he had shown himself to have good co-ordination and an eagle's eye so that during his army training he had often come top at target practice. In terms of accuracy he was adept with hand-guns and long-arms alike; but in both circumstances his habit was to hold the weapons at arm's length and take his time, armystyle. Plus, he had only ever used his right hand, which he naturally favoured for everyday activities. But all were limitations that could be lethal disadvantages in a face-to-face six-gun confrontation.

He now needed to build on his service experience. Particularly he needed to practise three skills that were new to him: a fast draw, using both hands, and firing from the hip.

For his pair of guns he had picked Army Colts with which he was familiar. But he had had to do things that he had never done before. Like, through trial and error, carving a piece out of the front of each holster to aid clearance; tying the base of each holster to his leg to reduce fumbling at the crucial time.

To remind his eyes and hands of their old skills he had begun by firing at the cans with arm stretched straight from the shoulder — successfully picking off the targets with no trouble. At first, he shot over a distance comparable to the army firing range that he had been used to, but then reminded himself that when it came to the crunch he was going to be much closer. Accordingly he moved the cans to within ten feet.

When the ground around his feet was littered with spent cases, he took the rounds from his guns and practised drawing as fast as he could, firing on empty chambers as soon as his gun was level.

Progressing to this stage he soon realized that, when he dropped his hands to his gun butts, it was imperative that he drew and fired — with no thinking. To draw and think would be fatal. Thus he had to develop the state of mind in which there would be no time for thinking once he had committed himself to drawing. The draw itself would be the signal to his brain that the sequence should be seen through to the end. He resolved to make that an iron rule and throughout his practice he consciously applied it.

Several times he caught the muzzle on the holster top and realized the gun was hung too high. He lowered the belt progressively till his hands fell naturally to the butts, with elbows only slightly bent. Then he practised drawing without hindering the barrel-end, first the right gun then the left.

In each case he let his hand hang loosely at his side then whipped the hand up to the pistol butt, catching the hammer under the thumb and sliding his forefinger into the trigger-guard. He would draw the gun, pulling back the hammer as he did so. He would tighten his grip on the butt as the gun cleared the holster, and pull the trigger as the muzzle became level.

He was clumsy at first, especially with his left hand, but he eventually got the hang of it. Finally he went through the process with live ammunition. During these later exercises he was less accurate than he had been when aiming at arm's length and taking his time. But, just as his clumsiness had lessened with practice, so did his accuracy improve. And he consoled himself that his targets were going to be larger than tin cans.

The second time he disposed of eight cans, drawing and firing simultaneously from both hips, he congratulated himself and sheathed his guns. Time for a break, he told himself, then another session or two should put him in the position of being able to go through the ritual as though it was second nature.

And there was something he was glad of: one ability he hadn't lost — that of being a quick learner, a quality his sergeant had praised on many an occasion.

★　★　★

It was mid-afternoon when the couple rode into Bullionville. They drew in at the first hitch rail in town.

'Stay here,' Savidge said, helping Holiday down from her horse. 'Look after the horses.'

He took Flying Dog's headband from his saddlebag and draped it over his shoulder.

'Joe, what are you going to do?'

They hadn't spoken of it before because she knew he wouldn't be drawn into detailed explanations, but she knew the answer to the question. She had watched him fuss over the set of guns he had bought in Pioche. She guessed that, when he had disappeared from The Overlander for long stretches since their return from the desert, he had found some place where he could practise gun dexterity, accuracy and fast draws. From what he had told her about his past, she knew that it had been a long time since he had used hand-guns in earnest and that he needed to brush the rust off his one-time skills. At such times she hadn't commented. She just hoped that whatever regime he had put himself through during his sessions on the outskirts of Pioche had been enough for the task he had set himself.

He kissed her cheek and said, 'You know what I'm going to do, gal. Just make sure you keep out of the way, is all.'

Her face distraught, Holiday watched him head along the drag, knowing that she had to do as he said and not interfere.

Outside The Eldorado he looked back once to check that she was staying well away. Then he pushed through the batwings and, standing in the doorway, took the place in. He ignored the handful of drinkers around the room. All he was concerned with were the three men seated at a table at the far end. He'd hoped the three he was after would be in there, and they were — Fage and his two henchmen. Three faces he could not forget.

Savidge went to the bar and ordered a large shot of whiskey. He dropped coins on the bar and took a sip. He removed his Stetson and carefully wrapped Flying Dog's band around his head, much to the curiosity of the onlookers. Then, glass in hand, he walked across the boards until he stood before the trio. 'It seems you don't like Indians.'

'You're darn right there, stranger,' Fage grunted.

'And you don't let them drink here.'

'You're right on that too. Smell the place up. But what the hell's it got to do with you?'

Savidge cast the remainder of the drink to the back of his throat and lobbed the empty glass on to their table where it rolled and dropped in Fage's lap.

'What the hell . . . ?' the gang boss spluttered, backhanding the dregs from his trousers and stumbling to his feet.

'Well, *I'm* an Indian,' the visitor said. 'And I've just had a drink in this shithole of yours. And you know what? I reckon I fancy another one. What you gonna do about it?'

The elderly Gelder appraised him slowly. 'You don't look like no redskin. And just wrapping a piece of cloth round your head don't make you one either.'

Savidge's forefinger briefly indicated his face. 'Maybe I got blue eyes,' he said, 'but look more closely at the features: the cheekbones and such. There's enough Indian showing through for even pissants like you to recognize. That's 'cos I'm a half-breed.'

'Well, we don't allow half-breeds in

here either,' Fage snarled. 'Fact, they're worse. Neither one thing or another.' He drew his gun. 'So get the hell out — while you can.'

Suddenly the young Turner pointed. 'Hey, I recognize him, boss. He's the bozo who butted in back a-whiles. You remember, the one whose ass we whupped and sent packing to Pioche on the back of that freighter's wagon.'

Fage peered. 'Him? Didn't think he'd make it after he'd took that battering with the butt of that Winchester. Must have a head of iron.' He squinted. 'Oh, yeah, it's the same feller. Didn't recognize him with them clean dude clothes and that primitive's rag round his head.' He looked at his pals and back at Savidge. 'So, 'breed, you got a chip on your shoulder and come back with an axe to grind?' he sneered. 'Figure we're gonna have ourselves another piece of fun here, boys.'

'Yeah, I got an axe to grind,' Savidge agreed, 'but not so much for me. Though you need paying back for that.

But more important: fact is, there's a widow in town needs some compensation — Flying Dog's widow. I've come to see you pay it.'

'What?' Fage chuckled in disbelief. 'You're asking for compensation for a dead injun?'

'Yeah. The man's name was Flying Dog — the man you killed — and this is his headband.'

'I don't believe this,' Fage sniggered. 'One against three?'

Savidge's eyes became more concentrated. 'You've got your gun out, use it.'

Fage shook his head in apparent disbelief. 'You can tell this guy's got Injun blood in him, can't you? He's an idiot. Let's show him, boys.'

With that he nodded a signal to his cronies and thumbed back the hammer on his own gun. His *compadres* took the cue and duly went for theirs.

There was a barrage of shots — from their guns and Savidge's.

As the deafening noise abated and the smoke cleared there were three men sprawled over chairs on the other side of the table. And Savidge had been hurled backwards so that he lay crumpled against the far wall. For a moment he didn't move. He groaned and eventually pulled himself slowly to his feet, pain writ large across his features. He leant, his back against the wall. He looked as though he was going to collapse, but he waved his smoke-tipped revolvers at the remaining occupants of the room.

'Listen up,' he said, in a voice that betrayed that it was an effort for him to speak. 'I've still got enough rounds left to sort out anybody else whose got objections.'

Someone said, 'No business of mine, pal.' Others echoed similar sentiments and a shuffling of feet indicated their indication to back off from any further action.

'How the hell did he pull that off?' one of the observers whispered out of the corner of his mouth to his friend. 'With three of them firing at him

— and Fage already had his gun in his hand! — they couldn't help but get at least one slug into him at that range.'

'I guess they did,' his companion muttered. 'Look at the state of him.'

Savidge shakily swung his gun in the direction of the bartender. 'And you?'

'Don't look at me,' the man said. 'You'll get no trouble from this quarter. I just work here.'

'Glad to hear it,' Savidge breathed. 'So just step back from the bar and away from whatever blaster you've got hidden there.' As the man did so, Savidge holstered one of his guns, keeping the remaining one levelled. He staggered across the boards and, laboriously, checked that the three fallen men had definitely breathed their last. He then proceeded to empty their pockets.

He walked slowly round the back of the bar and dropped the money that he had collected onto the counter. His hand explored beneath the bar and he withdrew the short-barrelled Sharps that he found hidden there. Shucking the loads from it, he cast the weapon aside, opened the till and pointed. 'Take out whatever wages are owed you,' he whispered to the barman. He took off the headband, spread it beside the till and dropped the money he had taken from the bodies onto it. 'Wrap the rest of the cash from the till in this and give it to me.'

While the bartender did as he was bid, Savidge returned the Stetson to his head.

Minutes later he was backing through the batwings, satisfied there would be no resistance.

Outside he came face to face with the constable.

'What's the ruckus all about, Joe?' the lawman wanted to know. 'For a moment I thought it was mine-blasting.'

'Hope I didn't wake you, Luke. No, there's been no mine-blasting. The noise you heard was just me persuading folk to pay their debts.'

The officer peered over the batwings, saw the bloody mayhem. 'They . . . they . . .'

'Yeah. They're as dead as they can be. Anything you want to do about it?'

The lawman absorbed the news, made his own judgements, then said, 'Well, looks like you did the town a good turn into the bargain.'

Savidge thumped his feet on the sand of the street and sat heavily on the boardwalk edge, breathing hard. He summoned up his strength and was pulling his shirt out of his pants when Holiday ran up to him. 'You're all right, Joe?'

'Yeah. Just help me get this thing off. It's chafing me raw.'

He pulled the shirt over his head to expose the Spanish breastplate he had come across at Vegas Wells. Together they undid the rawhide knots. She eased it off for him, noting the red weals where its edges had been rubbing against his flesh. When it was off he held it at arm's length for inspection. There were two shining new dents in it. He rubbed his fingers over the fresh depressions.

'The slugs didn't get through to me,'

he said, 'but, boy, I sure felt 'em!'

He dropped the breastplate on to the sand and pulled on his shirt.

'Is it all over?' she asked.

He nodded and picked up the bundled headband, hefting it so that it took the lawman's attention. 'Flying Dog's widow still living in the same shack at the end of town?'

'Yeah.'

'Got something here for her,' Savidge said, taking a roll of his own bills from a pocket and adding it to the makeshift bag.

'Where are we going now, Joe?' Holiday asked.

Savidge wrapped up the bundle once more and put his arm around her. 'Just gonna pay a call to drop this off . . . and then we go wherever you say.'

She nestled against his chest. 'I'm real proud of you, Joe.'

'Yes,' he continued. 'We go wherever you say — that is once we've stopped by a store and stocked up with some canned peaches.'

HELL FIRE IN PARADISE

Chuck Tyrell

Laurel Baker lost her husband and her two boys on the same day. Then, menacingly, logging magnate Robert Dunn rides into her ranch on Paradise Creek to buy her out. Laurel refuses as her loved ones are buried there — prompting Dunn to try shooting to get his way. Laurel's friends stick by her, but will their loyalty match Dunn's ten deadly gunmen? And in the final battle for her land, can she live through hell fire in Paradise?

THE BLACK MOUNTAIN DUTCHMAN

Steve Ritchie

In Wyoming, when Maggie Buckner is captured by a gang of outlaws, 'the Dutchman' is the only one who can free her. Near Savage Peak, the old man adjusts the sights on his Remington No. 1 rifle as the riders come into range. When he stops shooting, three of the captors lay dead. After striking the first deadly blows, the Dutchman trails the group across South Pass like the fourth horseman of the apocalypse . . . and surely Hell follows with him.

THE FIGHTING MAN

Alan Irwin

Young Rob Sinclair, a homesteader's son in the Wyoming Territory, has never handled a gun. But when the Nolan gang kills his parents, he's determined to bring the culprits to justice. Against the prevailing knowledge that only a real fighting man could defeat the Nolan gang, Rob learns to fight and sets out to search for the killers. He eventually reaches the Texas Panhandle, little knowing what awaits him there. Can he complete such a perilous mission alone?

BLOOD FEUD

John Dyson

Higo, a Japanese railroad worker, kills two guards and escapes into Utah's canyonlands, and when Cal Mitchell goes after him — it's not just for the $500 reward . . . Along with his tempestuous passion for Modesty, dark secrets beckon Cal homeward, towards the mountains of Zion. He also seeks vengeance against the five Granger brothers. Blood flows and bullets fly as Cal steps back into his murky past. Can he find peace when the odds are stacked against him?

COLTAINE'S REVENGE

Scott Connor

Lewis Coltaine had wanted vengeance and tracked down Emerson Greeley, his wife's murderer. But Emerson promised Lewis that even after his death, he would find no peace. And when he returned home Emerson's threat had come to pass. His eldest brother had been murdered. Now, the surviving brothers vow to find the man responsible. However, the clues point to a dark, long-buried family secret, which could tear the family apart. Can Lewis Coltaine finally deliver his revenge?

BLOOD ON THE SAND

Lee Lejeune

Mav, on his way west from Tennessee, encounters a gang of desperadoes about to kill a young Apache brave. When he intervenes to save the victim he stirs up a lot of bad blood — but he also forges an unusual partnership when a band of Comanche comes to his aid. He rides on the small town of Cimmaron hoping, at last, to find some rest . . . but he soon discovers that there are more surprises left in store for him yet . . .